ASHOAN'

T0166396

At the center of these stories is a hatchlu prayer rug, whose wide row of deep Vs is "like strong bird wings flying." The workmanship in the rug is "tight and beautiful." Both of those descriptions fit the book itself—a rich, intricate, finely structured weaving of narratives that transport the reader across decades and continents. Each story is so convincing and moving, I had to stop and catch my breath before I could turn to the next, allowing it to work its magic, just as the rug brought magic into the lives of these characters.
Judy Goldman, author of *Losing My Sister*

Part *La Ronde* and part *Tales from the Arabian Nights*, Knowles' *Ashoan's Rug* is a charming flight through time and space. It is a tapestry of memorable characters, employing beautifully layered dialogue and situations just implausible enough to be truly real.
Ian Finley, playwright

Carrie Knowles is a talented story weaver who knows how to thread a golden tale filled with magic, beauty and emotion. Like a flying carpet, *Ashoan's Rug* will lift you off the page and take you on an incredible and unforgettable journey.
Maureen Sherbondy, author of *The Slow Vanishing*

Knowles' ability to weave ten tight, superb stories into a magnificent tapestry is nothing short of magic.
Jodi Barnes, author/editor of the blog, Worker Writes

Ashoan's Rug

Ashoan's Rug

Carrie Jane Knowles

Winchester, UK
Washington, USA

First published by Roundfire Books, 2013
Roundfire Books is an imprint of John Hunt Publishing Ltd., Laurel House, Station Approach,
Alresford, Hants, SO24 9JH, UK
office1@jhpbooks.net
www.johnhuntpublishing.com
www.roundfire-books.com

For distributor details and how to order please visit the 'Ordering' section on our website.

Text copyright: Carrie Jane Knowles 2013

ISBN: 978 1 78279 112 6

A CIP catalogue record for this book is available from the British Library.

Design: Lee Nash

Printed and bound by CPI Group (UK) Ltd, Croydon, CR0 4YY

We operate a distinctive and ethical publishing philosophy in all
areas of our business, from our global network of authors to
production and worldwide distribution.

This book is dedicated to Jeff, Neil, Hedy and Cole.
You believed in me and never once hesitated to come along for the
ride and the dream.
Thank you.

Acknowledgements

I would like to thank Peggy Payne, Ingrid Wood and Sue Shoemaker for their comments, encouragement and careful reading of this manuscript.

I would also like to thank Quail Ridge Books for their many years of supporting and believing in the value of the long creative road to a finished book.

Bless you and all the other bookstores in the world!

The work of any art is not in the creation, but in how the artwork changes lives.

CHAPTER 1

1894
THE RUG

"Seda," Lala sobbed, curling her body into a tight ball as the next contraction ripped across her stomach, "something is wrong. My baby has been quiet now for two days."

Seda stroked the back of the girl's head with her right hand and placed her left hand flat on the side of the girl's big stomach.

"The moon was resting," Seda said. "The baby was resting too."

Seda pressed her hand hard against the girl's side to see if the baby would move. "Breathe with me," Seda commanded while she pushed and kneaded the tight belly. "Together we will wake this baby and help it travel into this world."

Three moons ago, Seda had held two stillborn babies and sung the death song to them, touching their tiny closed eyelids in order to give them messages to carry to their ancestors in the next world. They were twin girls who would not have made it even if they had managed to fall screaming from their mother's loins. They were just too small to survive.

This baby, however, was big. Seda could feel the broad sole of its foot push against her hand as she tried to wake it in its mother's womb. She felt certain it would live, as long as Lala didn't panic and its journey here could be ridden on the loving songs of the women waiting to catch it, not the screams of its anxious mother.

"Is your rug almost finished?" Seda asked Lala. Yesterday she had seen the girl sitting with the women weaving and had noticed her shoulders slumped uncomfortably around her big stomach as she worked slowly over the pattern of her rug.

"I have the skirt to weave yet, and to tie it off."

"Ashoan will finish it for you," Seda said. She placed her hands on either side of the girl's belly so she could massage its tight expanse. As she worked her fingers she could feel the soft curl of the baby's back along the dark hairline down Lala's stomach and the large crown of the baby's head pushing down into the girl's small hips. The baby was turned and ready but there was no longer any room for it to move.

"This baby is big. He wants to get out and we must help him."

"Too big?" Lala wailed. "So big he will split me open like a melon the way Hasad did his mother?"

Seda closed her eyes so she could concentrate on her hands. Lala had always been a silly girl and now Seda feared she would be an equally silly mother.

"I will call upon our ancestors. We will need their help. It is a big job to go from one world to the next. The baby is resting now. He is preparing himself to come. You must prepare yourself also. Ashoan," Seda called out to her daughter, "it is Lala's time. Gather the women for me."

Ashoan poked her head into her mother's tent. Ashoan was a season older than Lala, but no one had claimed her for his bride. Her hands were not as quick as the other girls' at weaving, and her right eye and cheek were blemished with a deep purple mark, like the welt a hand might leave on a face if someone slapped it. Ashoan quickly turned her marked cheek away when Lala looked at her.

"I shall tell them," Ashoan said obediently.

"And, Ashoan," her mother added, "once the women have drawn the water and the fire is built for the night, you must go and finish Lala's weaving. Be swift. The rug should be cut from the loom before the baby's first cry."

Seda knew the omens were not good when babies came on unfinished business. Ashoan had come in the middle of a rug, and Seda had no desire to tempt the Fates so soon after the stillborn twins. It was unclear to Seda whether Ashoan had

2

rushed to come before the rug was finished and that is what marked her face and slowed her hands, or if Seda's own slowness to finish her rug had damaged her baby. These were not questions any of them could answer.

"It will be done," Ashoan swore to her mother, and she left the tent.

While she wove on Lala's rug by the firelight, Ashoan could hear the women singing through Lala's screams. As the fearful wailing of Lala rose, the singing of the women climbed as well. Higher and higher the younger women's voices ascended while the older ones hummed a low droning call like waves rolling out to sea then crashing against a ragged shore. Ashoan closed her tired eyes and let the music carry her slow fingers across Lala's dull little rug.

"If this were my rug," Ashoan sang softly as she worked, "I would weave into it the red of fire. If this were my rug, the stitches would be tight and straight. If this were my rug it would be beautiful."

Although she was nearly fifteen and more than old enough, Ashoan had not yet been given her own rug to weave. Her hands had been slower than the other girls' at learning the knots, but now her knots were strong and sure. She had proven herself on her mother's loom. Several months ago her mother had promised her a rug to weave. But, after the stillborn twins had come, her mother had said they must wait until the smell of death had left their camp and the wind blew fresh again.

As Ashoan worked she listened carefully to the singing of the women. Their voices were growing louder, and the pounding, droning cadence shook the earth like a wild galloping horse. The sound, Ashoan knew, was the baby straining to push its way into this world. Ashoan begged her hands to move faster, the fine threads of the rug skirt rolling in her fingers, wrapping and knotting their way across the warp on the loom. She knew the baby must not come before the rug was cut free from the loom.

"If this were my rug," she sang as she worked her hands from knot to knot, "my husband would not sell it. He would praise me for its beauty. When I cut it from the loom, the weaving women would take hold of its long silken fringe and dance around the fire."

The droning pulsed through the chilled night air. "Al-lah, Al-lah, Al-lah," it seemed to call out beckoning for help to bring the baby home.

Ashoan worked faster.

"Al-lah, Al-lah," the voices of the old women pulsed and pushed the baby forward. She could hear Lala scream.

"My rug will be beautiful," Ashoan sang to herself, letting her own voice rise a little as she took her sharp knife and twisted each knotted fringe in order to cut it free in one clean stroke. Twist, cut, twist, cut, her fingers worked their way from one end of the loom to the other.

"Al-lah, Al-lah," came the drone.

When she finished with the bottom fringe, Ashoan stood to cut the rug free from the other end of the loom.

"My rugs will bring me riches," she sang, her body swaying to the music of the women in the birthing tent. "My husband will be proud."

"EEEEEE-yah!" came the sharp deafening cry from Seda.

"A son!" Ashoan heard her mother call out to the men waiting in the shadows. "Lala, the good wife, gives her husband a son. Hear him cry."

Seda dipped the newborn boy's heels in a pan of cold water and he cried out, and as he did, Seda quickly cut the cord binding him to his mother and the other world. The women who had been holding Lala's shaking legs began massaging her belly to bring the afterbirth.

Before Seda had finished her song of life to the baby and wrapped him in a shawl and pushed his searching mouth to

Lala's small breast, Ashoan was standing at the door of the tent with the rug rolled in her arms.

"It was cut before he cried," she said, her face beaming.

Seda examined the fine tight knots her daughter had made in Lala's poorly woven rug.

"You brought luck to Lala's baby on his journey here and beauty to her rug. Good work, my daughter."

"The smell of death has been swept from our camp," Ashoan said boldly.

"The baby cried out strong. He will live."

"The wind blows fresh."

"The wind blows fresh," Seda replied, touching her daughter's darkened cheek. "Come and sit by the fire with me and let us dream," she said, taking Ashoan's hands. "We have worked hard tonight, the two of us, to bring this baby safely here. We are tired, but not so tired we cannot dream a fine rug for you."

"It must be more than the tiny saddle-blanket Lala has woven for her son."

"A good rug."

"A beautiful rug," Ashoan sang out as she danced towards the fire.

"A beautiful rug," her mother answered. "Come sit."

Obediently, Ashoan sat next to her mother and waited. Her mother pulled her shawl from her shoulders and brought it up over her head like a tent. She crossed her arms over her chest, letting the shawl nearly cover her face.

Ashoan closed her eyes and let the embers of the night fire warm her tired hands and bare feet.

Her mother began to rock and hum. It was not like the pulsing humming of the drones, but instead it was a quiet hum like a far off flapping of great wings. As Seda hummed she let her mind fly over the life of her daughter. She opened her heart to the whispers of the spirits. She kept her face covered because she knew what she saw would bring tears to her eyes. She knew she would not see a tall strong husband for Ashoan like Lala's. Just as her daughter's face was marked, her life was marked as well.

Ashoan was getting older. Seda had long since given up hoping some strong young man would come for Ashoan. For Ashoan, it would be an old stooped widower who wished for warmth at night and a woman who could weave for him and spin wool into gold.

Seda brought her forehead close to her knees as she hummed and rocked her body into a tight ball. Seda feared the mark on Ashoan's face would make her husband cruel. She was also aware her daughter's fingers would be sure but slow on the loom and her husband might become impatient with her. Her daughter's life would surely be harsh. Seda's heart ached for Ashoan's simple spirit and her trusting eyes.

Ashoan waited patiently. She knew not to touch her mother or to try to wake her from her song. She too could hear the spirits whispering in the cool night air.

Ashoan got up twice to bring more dung for the fire. She could hear the women singing softly in the tent for Lala's new son. She could hear them weave their story about how strong her baby was, how quick to find the tit to nurse, how handsome the baby was, just like his father. She knew they were working while they sang, braiding Lala's freshly washed hair. The men on the other side of the fire huddled around Lala's husband, slapping him on the back telling him how lucky he was to marry a beautiful woman such as Lala who could so soon after his wedding night bring him a strong screaming son.

Seda hugged her knees as her mind flew. She could see the old man who would come to take Ashoan from their tribe. His face was not disfigured, but it held no kindness. He would not look at Ashoan when he took his pleasure. He would trade her rugs without touching them, or without ever singing of their beauty.

Only Ashoan would sing for them. Only Ashoan would touch them with love and care.

The dusky smoke of the dung fire clung to Seda's shawl and stung her covered eyes. She could also see Ashoan's rug. She reached out, scooped up a handful of sand, brought it to her lips and kissed it in thanks to the spirit who had come to help her. She threw the sand into the hissing fire. Sparks flew.

Seda quietly lifted her shawl away from her face and let it fall to her shoulders.

"I see a fine rectangular rug with a tight weave. You must weave it with a hatchlu, a cross within its center to draw the spirits close to you wherever you make your home. This rug should be big enough to be a door for your tent and keep your home warm. But, not so big that you cannot easily roll it up and tie it to your camel."

"Yes," Ashoan said, closing her eyes and imagining the wonderful rug, "I must weave a hatchlu design. A good omen."

Seda smoothed the small patch of sand between her daughter and herself and drew a neat oblong shape in it with her finger.

"A hatchlu with two strong columns of birds flying on either side, their wings spread like this."

Seda drew a series of wide opened Vs with her fingers down the two sides of the rug.

"These wings will carry you over your troubles."

"Troubles cannot harm you if you are carried over them with wings so beautiful," Ashoan proudly announced, her fingers touching the fine lines her mother had drawn.

"Along the straight line of the hatchlu marking the entrance to your tent there will be two lines of camels to carry your load."

"Yes," Ashoan whispered, "camels to carry my husband's tent and my loom with me wherever we go."

"And here, you will weave a small mahrib. Not so big as anyone would notice, but a fine delicate design. A secret you will weave into the rug. A place for you to rest your head and pray so

CHAPTER 2

1910
THE MERCHANT

Akmed was sick of the smell of rotting fruit, excrement, sweating bodies, and the burnt nauseating aroma of roasting coffee beans swirling all around him like flies in the blasted heat of Istanbul. This had not been a good buying trip, and it had not been a good day. The late afternoon temperatures had steadily risen faster than his small stack of rugs, forcing him to remember once again how much he hated the bazaar and why he came there only because he had to. He always prayed his business would not take long. Even one day was too long to spend in the heat and dust of the stinking bazaar. He'd already been in Istanbul two weeks and had little to show for his efforts.

He couldn't wait to pack up and get back to London where everyone bathed at least once a week and people didn't urinate like animals in the streets.

"Sweet Allah," he said, wiping the sweat from his face with the dusty edge of his sleeve, "bring me more rugs so I can go back to my room and get out of this furnace of damnation."

It was a foolish prayer. A selfish one he knew should not be answered. He ached to leave his place among the other rug buyers, but knew he couldn't go, at least not yet. This was the last day he would be there, and he needed at least twenty more rugs before he could begin the three-week journey back to his shop in London.

Twenty more rugs could seem like an eternity when they came so pitifully one at a time. He kicked his little pile of rugs with the toe of his slipper, counting them as he kicked. Twelve today. Twelve added to the sixty-five he had in his room. Seventy-seven. All he had managed in two weeks of sitting in this wretched bazaar throwing money at the weavers was seventy-seven rugs, not enough to have made the long journey worthwhile. He needed at least a hundred. Two hundred would be better, but two hundred would be too many to hope for right now in this heat and so late in his stay. He wished to be back home in London, sitting in the shade of his alleyway drinking a cup of English tea with a lump of sugar in his cheek to sweeten it.

This trip was cursed from the start. The boat had been slowed by a storm. When he at last arrived, his favorite guesthouse was full, forcing him to stay at another much smaller and dirtier place closer to the sounds and the smells of the bazaar. His body ached from the foul lumpy mattress and the resulting lack of sleep. He closed his eyes in the hopes of trying to get just one blessed minute of rest.

"Allah be praised," he said, rocking gently back and forth in his whispered prayers, remembering how full and beautiful his little shop had looked with the three hundred rugs he'd managed from his last trip, all rolled out on the floor and stacked along the walls.

But, that was five years ago when rugs were plentiful and there were not so many other merchants bargaining for them. That was also before the workshops were set up in the cities like little factories and the weavers and their children came to work everyday to make rugs for somebody else, not themselves. There were so many cheap rugs to sell and so many people who wanted to buy them his life was made miserable trying to sell only the best. Even the rich people from America, weren't interested in the best. Instead, they wanted the cheapest. It was a terrible way to do a good business.

Akmed stopped rocking and opened his eyes. More sellers were coming towards him. Their animals were loaded with rugs, but the men did not look tired and hungry. They looked refreshed as though they had just come from the cafes or had recently taken a bath. He knew they brought cheap rugs from the puddings.

The sun was beginning to go down. Akmed could hear the other rug merchants finishing their business and packing away the fat bundles of rugs they'd purchased today. He closed his eyes for another moment and prayed for a breath of fresh air and one more weaver to come his way.

When he opened his eyes, Ashoan was standing before him.

"You bring me rugs," he said, not as a question but as an affirmation as to why she was standing there before him.

Ashoan pulled the scarf she was wearing on her head over her scarred cheek.

"Where is your husband, woman?" he asked, looking around, hoping the husband was not far away and ready to unload this burden of rugs.

Ashoan turned her head and nodded.

Akmed looked down the dusty road and saw an old man coming their way. His walk was crooked and unsteady. He was twice the age of the woman standing before him and his face was hard and deeply rutted. Akmed looked at Ashoan. She turned away and cast her eyes down to the ground.

"Let me see your hands," Akmed commanded.

As if she had been asked and had done so for strangers a hundred times before, Ashoan held her hands out with her palms up. Slowly, she turned them palms down so he could examine her fingernails.

Ashoan's hands were cracked and calloused, her nails ragged and stained with dye.

"I would like to see your beautiful rugs," he said, watching as the old man approached.

Ashoan stood perfectly still, like an animal afraid any sudden move might invoke the wrath of the owner and provoke a beating.

"You have met my beautiful wife," the old man shouted as he approached. "Uncover your cheek," he commanded Ashoan, "so he might see the burden you carry for both of us."

Ashoan turned her face toward Akmed and let her scarf drop for a moment, revealing the thick crimson scar covering her cheek and touching the edge of her right eye. Akmed did not look away.

"A real beauty, eh?" the old man sneered.

"There is beauty there," Akmed said, angry he had waited all day in the heat to meet such a man, "as there is beauty in the rugs she weaves."

"Ah, the rugs. My beautiful wife's beautiful rugs. How did you guess?"

"She has the eyes of a dreamer and the hands of a weaver."

The old man slapped the rear end of his camel and the bony beast sat down in a heap. Ashoan let the lead rope drop and turned to the business of untying the rugs.

"Since you are the only merchant still sitting here in the shadows of this hot day I assume you are the one who is interested in finding the finest of rugs, not the cheap ones made in the workshops, but the magic ones woven by moonlight. Isn't that what you tell your rich customers?"

"I tell them I buy only the best."

"The best does not come cheap."

"I would not expect," Akmed said, getting up and dusting off his robes.

Ashoan untied the rugs one at a time and after she untied each, she unrolled them on the ground in front of Akmed and smoothed the soft nap with her hands. The reds were dark and rich, the blacks like charred wood and the whites a soft cream color like desert sand. Akmed did not need to stoop and touch the rugs in order to feel the strength of the knots Ashoan had tied in them. His eyes could see what she had so carefully woven. His nose could smell the faint wisp of campfire smoke and the crushed wildflowers she used to dye her yarn. He ran the toe of his slipper across the large soft red rug before him and let the silken hand of it shiver up his leg.

"The work is beautiful."

"I've seen better," Akmed lied.

The old man snapped his fingers and Ashoan bent down and began rolling and tying the rugs she had just spread onto the ground.

"Stop!" Akmed shouted.

The old man nodded his head and Ashoan resumed untying the rugs. The two men stood in silence while Ashoan worked. Akmed moved from rug to rug as Ashoan laid out each new one.

Akmed stood by one of the larger ones, a double-hooked "T" motif flanking each side, a beautiful hatchlu design in the center. He nodded his head toward the old man.

"How much?"

"Depends," he said tilting his head to the side, "my camel is tired. He does not want to carry these rugs any further, and you look to be the only merchant."

"I want to see them all."

Ashoan continued unfolding the rugs. Akmed stood watching, his arms crossed, signaling there would be no further discussion until all of them were spread before him. Ashoan worked as fast as she could, looking over at her husband each time she returned to the camel to untie another until all were untied and unrolled except one.

"All of them," Akmed commanded, noting the one still left on the camel. He counted the rugs with his eyes. There were twenty before him. One more would make twenty-one, and with the seventy-seven he already had, would have ninety-eight rugs and could happily pack up and go home.

Ashoan hesitated. Her husband narrowed his eyes and jerked his head toward the camel. Ashoan moved to the camel and began untying the knot on the last rug as slowly as she dared.

"This last rug will cost you," the old man said, watching Akmed as Ashoan unrolled the beautiful hatchlu rug. Like the others, it too had a double-hooked "T" motif down each side, and a wide row of deep Vs, like strong bird wings flying up each side and a delicate geometric floral motif in the quadrants of the cross in the center of the rug. The workmanship was tight and beautiful. The rich burnt red, blacks, browns and tans were accented with a faint touch of bright red. It was like all the other rugs she had unrolled before him, but different in a way he could not name. He bent to touch it.

"A wedding gift," the old man chuckled.

Ashoan flinched.

Akmed did not like the old man.

"A beauty," Akmed said, looking up at Ashoan. She turned her face away.

"Ah, so the scar on my wife's cheek does not frighten you. But you have not seen it in the middle of the night, or in the first light of the morning. It is like a bad dream that won't go away."

"Some of us manage to keep our scars hidden, others are not so lucky. Yours seems to be a stiff leg causing you to walk like you are drunk."

The old man narrowed his eyes and glared at Akmed.

Akmed ignored him.

"Name your price," Akmed said, walking from rug to rug, kicking them with the toe of his shoe as he passed each one.

"For the rugs or my wife?"

Ashoan covered her face and turned away from the two men.

Akmed pretended not to hear the man's question.

The old man spun around and hit Ashoan hard across the back of her head. She stumbled before she fell to the ground. By the way she fell and gathered her skirts around her legs Akmed knew it was the not the first time she had been hit. He also knew it wouldn't be the last.

Akmed turned his head away. Living in London all these years had changed Akmed's mind about women. He had never hit his own wife and he wished for his daughters that their husbands would not hit them either.

"Do not hit her again," Akmed cautioned.

"She is my wife and I can hit her if I want. I can sell her if I want. She is no more than this camel to me. If you want her, take her, but you will pay dearly for her rugs."

"I am here to buy rugs," Akmed said quietly, "not to take another man's wife."

He watched as Ashoan staggered to get on her feet. She moved as far away as she dared, and sat down on the ground, her head bowed so it touched her knees and her face could not be seen.

"Eight hundred," the old man proclaimed with a wild sweeping gesture of his hand.

It was a high price, but a price Akmed knew he could easily triple in his little shop.

"Six," Akmed shot back.

"Seven for the rugs and another hundred for my wife."

Akmed was tired of this old man. He wanted him to take his camel and his wife and go away.

"You do not want my wife? Apparently, you do not understand the bargain here. I said seven hundred for the rugs and another hundred for my wife."

"I have a wife. I do not need yours."

"Your wife is in London dreaming of another man's face tonight. You have no wife here."

Akmed narrowed his eyes and turned his head toward Ashoan. He neither wanted her nor wanted to hurt her.

"So," the old man smiled, "now you are interested."

"All of the rugs, including the last one."

"All of them."

Akmed walked down the row of rugs spread at his feet. They were beautiful, the best he had ever seen. They would not last long in his little shop. The richest customers, the ones with the greedy eyes would pick them out even before they were unrolled. These rugs would make him a wealthy man and he would buy his wife a pair of beautiful emerald earrings.

"You will insult me if you do not take my wife."

Akmed considered what the man was saying. If he was to have the rugs he was going to have to take his wife.

"I am leaving tomorrow," he said, reaching into his caftan to bring out his satchel of money.

"And so, you will sleep well tonight."

"I am tired."

The old man turned toward Ashoan and motioned for her to roll up the rugs and put them back on the camel.

"Seven hundred," Akmed said, loosening the strings on his purse, "a fair price for such beautiful rugs."

"And a hundred for my wife for one night."

The old man's eyes were cruel and cold. Akmed knew the old man wished more to hurt his wife than to sell her rugs. He wondered how many times the woman had had to untie the rugs and unroll them only to have to pick them up again and move on to the next customer who refused to pay to sleep with her because she was ugly.

"Fifty," Akmed said. The word felt sharp and salty in his mouth like a slap across the face and he instantly regretted it. Ashoan flinched.

"I believe she is worth more," the sly old man said as he stooped to roll up the last rug Ashoan had taken from the camel's saddle.

Akmed watched as he rolled up the prized rug. It was the best and they both knew it. He could ask five times what he paid for it and get it easily.

"A hundred for one night. She must be a very special wife."

"She will do whatever you ask. She is a simple woman."

More than anything Akmed wanted these rugs so he could go home where his own wife would be waiting.

"Do we have a bargain?" the old man patted the rolled-up rug in his arms as though it were a sleeping baby.

"You will carry the rugs to my hotel. As I said before, I am departing in the morning. Where should I leave your wife?"

"She will find me."

Ashoan got up from where she was sitting and began rolling the rugs and tying them onto the camel again. She took her time and made each bundle a tight one so she could carry more than five at a time and would therefore have fewer trips to make up the stairs of the hotel.

Akmed counted the money into the old man's hands. When the transaction was done, Akmed led the way. Ashoan and the old man followed with the camel and the rugs. When they arrived at the hotel, Ashoan once again untied each rug and carried them in bundles up the stairs to Akmed's room.

The night air was thick and humid. Akmed opened the windows of the room and looked out into the street below.

"Bring us some food," he said to Ashoan, handing her a few of coins from his velvet money pouch.

"What would you like?" she asked as she held out her hand to take the coins.

"I am too tired and hungry to care. Get whatever you want."

Ashoan left with the money.

Akmed had paid for Ashoan and he knew she must do whatever he asked. It had been weeks since he had shared a bed with his wife. Too many weeks sleeping first on a tossing ship, and now on this lumpy hot mattress. A woman's hands to rub his sore shoulders would feel good. It would be foolish to throw good money away.

When Ashoan came back to the room with a half-dozen small bundles of food, she took the rug, the one that had been the wedding gift, unrolled it onto the floor and began opening the small bundles she'd bought. She spread the food out over the rug as though she were setting out a feast in the desert.

"Take off your clothes," Akmed commanded as he tore a piece of bread and picked up a lump of cheese.

Ashoan slowly removed her headscarf, shook out her hair and undid the shoulders of her robe in order to let it slip to the floor. She stepped away from the crumpled garment and began to move shyly around the little rug in her camisole and pantaloons.

Akmed watched her dance. The skin that had been covered by her robes was white as milk while her hands and feet were stained like old wood from work and walking. As she twisted and twirled around him, her dark stained hands became two brightly plumed birds stirring the cool air of the evening.

All Akmed could look at were her beautiful stained hands. All he could think about was having her hands fluttering across his body. Ashoan began to hum.

"Take off your clothes," Akmed said again as he unfastened his caftan.

Ashoan stepped gingerly around the rug and as she moved, she slowly lifted her camisole. When it was free of her body and held high over her head she turned toward Akmed so he could look at her.

Akmed cursed.

Her belly was as big and tight as a summer melon.

She untied her pantaloons.

Akmed turned his head.

"Put them back on," he barked.

Ashoan quickly pulled the camisole back over her head and stretched it safely over her stomach, letting her hands caress the smooth crest of her growing baby. She retied her pantaloons and walked over to put on her dress.

"Your husband is a cruel man," Akmed said as he tore another piece of bread and filled it with olives and cheese.

Ashoan did not speak. Her face was tight with fear.

"Sit with me," he said softly, "and eat."

Ashoan did as commanded.

Akmed watched her eat. He tore another piece of bread and

stuffed it with cheese. He did not like being cheated. The old man's words, "She will do whatever you ask," buzzed and rattled like angry wasps in his head. He tried to push his anger away. His anger was not with her; it was with her husband.

"Tell me about this rug," he said.

Ashoan looked down at the rug as though she hadn't seen it for a very long time, a lifetime ago. She wiped her right hand on the front of her dress and let her fingers trace the pattern along the border. She opened her broad hand and placed her palm against the small mahrib and bowed her head for a moment and hummed quietly to herself.

"This was my first rug," Ashoan began.

Akmed took a handful of dates from one of the little bundles Ashoan had set out on the rug. He offered one to Ashoan. She took it.

"Tell me," he said, putting his head in her lap, "about this rug." He took one of the plump dates and popped it into his mouth and gently bit down on it. He let the sweet juice from the date fill his mouth while he waited for her to speak.

Ashoan's baby-belly rocked against the crown of Akmed's head. She was humming as she rocked. Akmed waited.

"My mother dreamed this rug for me," she whispered.

"Tell me the story," he said, letting his empty hand reach down to touch the edge of the tightly woven skirt of her beautiful little rug.

Ashoan closed her eyes. She started to sing the song her mother always sang when she sat down at her loom to weave. Her careful voice filled the room. The baby that was growing inside of her womb fluttered.

"Here," she said taking Akmed's hand in hers, "are the flowers I wove to soothe my tired fingers at the end of the day and to bring peace to my heart and my home. And here," she said moving his hand over a little to the left where the wide spread Vs were like the strong flapping wings of great birds, "are the birds

22

I imagined would carry my troubles away."

Akmed closed his eyes and tried to feel the beating wings of the birds as Ashoan talked and sang her way across the rug and through the night. It was as if her rug was magic and they were not resting in this hot room anymore, but flying through a cool evening breeze high above the world and he could see the campfire where she had been when she wove her rug and could hear the songs she had heard.

Akmed had never felt anything like this before and when sleep finally came to him it filled him like a strong sweet wine. Several times throughout the night he struggled to open his eyes but failed. Day and night were spinning together and he no longer cared whether or not he could tell if Ashoan was singing or he was merely dreaming a beautiful wind song. Sometimes his hand touched the edge of the world and sometimes it brushed against the edge of her beautiful rug.

When the sun at last came up, he was surprised to discover he was not out in the desert listening to the songs of the cool night wind, but back in his hot little room in Istanbul.

The rug was on the floor, and Ashoan was gone.

CHAPTER 3

1914
THE BOY

Angel was twelve years old and he was blind. He had soft gray eyes, however, that flickered nervously from one object to another like radar, as if he could see. When he was born, his father, Mr. Horace Crittenden II, had been so repulsed by the child's strange blind eyes he told the doctor it was hard for him to believe anything so unformed and odd like Angel could grow to be a real man.

Angel's mother, on the other hand, thought he was simply beautiful and she loved him fiercely. When her husband refused to name him Horace, she had named him Angel.

"I CAN see," Angel told her when he felt her staring at him. He was sitting by the window looking out into the street. His mother was sitting a few feet away watching him.

"It's fine," she answered, ashamed she had once again been wishing he was a normal child and could see.

"I CAN, in my right eye. There's a bright shaft of light and sometimes dancing things."

"Shadows," she said, smoothing the front of her dress as she got up from the chair to go into her husband's office in the back of the house.

"Will you tell father?" he begged.

"Yes," she promised, "I will."

She moved from the room with an air of confidence. There were certain moments when Mrs. Horace Crittenden wondered how or why she had ever gotten married to someone as unimaginative as Horace, but whenever she had these thoughts she comforted herself with the knowledge he was rich and could give her

24

anything she fancied. Unlimited wealth, her mother once told her, lasted longer than love and was reason enough to marry the dullest of men.

Mrs. Crittenden really had no intention of trying to tell Horace his son believed he could see shadows. She had more important things to discuss with her husband.

"Horace," she called out as she brushed through the doorway of his office into the center of the room, "I've had this splendid idea. I think Angel and I should go to Europe. We'll take the boat from New York to London. From there we'll travel to Paris and points south."

"Points south?" he questioned as he moved toward his desk.

"Venice, Rome, then on to Greece. He would be so excited to see the ruins."

Horace didn't answer her immediately. Instead, he turned his back on her and started shuffling through a stack of papers on the top of his desk. He hated her talking about Angel "seeing" this and "seeing" that as though taking him away from Boston gave him sight.

"He loves all those Greek stories," she said, sensing Horace's annoyance.

"You mean the myths," he shot back.

"Myths," she said impatiently, knowing she was being criticized for being imprecise.

"You can't travel alone."

"We'll take Martha. She's terribly good with Angel; he loves her so."

"How long?"

"The agency suggested three, maybe four months. The passage takes time. They'll handle all the arrangements. The European trains are very reliable."

"Four months? What in God's name is there for a child like Angel to see in all of Europe that such a voyage would take four months?"

"There's everything," Mrs. Horace Crittenden snapped, "everything in the world."

"When do you plan on leaving?"

"Two weeks from Thursday."

"Hardly time enough to do the paperwork," he snorted.

"It's already done," Mrs. Crittenden announced with a flourish as she turned away from him and went out the door.

The passage from New York to London was long and arduous. Angel's governess, Martha, had never traveled by ship before and had been sick at first then afterwards, downright scared to death she might never live to see land again. When she wasn't hanging over the railing losing her last meal and gasping for fresh air, she was in her darkened cabin on her knees praying.

Martha's fear and seasickness left Mrs. Crittenden in charge of everything, including Angel.

Angel, quite fortunately, was not sick. He was, however, fascinated by the big ship, so when she wasn't taking care of Martha, Mrs. Crittenden walked the decks with him so he could explore.

"It feels so smooth and cool," Angel said as his hand came to rest on the edge of a large brass fitting, his fingers skimming the shiny surface like a flicker of light. "Could I press my cheek against it?"

Mrs. Crittenden took a moment to think about what it was Angel wanted to do, and also to think about what Martha would say if Angel had asked her the same thing. She looked around to see if anyone was watching. One of the stewards was walking along the deck.

"In a moment," she said, moving closer to the object in question in order to provide some cover for him.

"Tell me when it's safe."

"Now," she said, once the steward was long past them. She was surprised to feel her heart race with excitement.

"Have you ever known anything this beautiful before?" Angel asked.

"No," she said, as Angel rubbed his cheek against the sun-warmed metal. Watching him made her reflect on how Angel found so much pleasure yet wanted so little from the world around him. He was not at all like his father who wanted everything.

"It is a marvelous boat."

"Yes," she answered, and tugged at his sleeve. "We'd better move on before we get caught."

They walked together exploring the boat for about an hour. When she grew weary, she asked the steward for two deck chairs and two lap robes. Once situated, she and Angel sat together in silence for a long time enjoying the warmth of the sun on their faces and the ruffle of the cool breeze as the boat cut slowly through the water towards England. It was, she thought, a most pleasant way to spend an afternoon, much better by far than being trapped at home in stuffy old Boston.

She had brought her book with her and hoped Angel would soon drift off to sleep so she might have some time to herself to read.

"Tell me a story," he said, touching her arm.

"Ahh, a story," she replied lazily, "let me see, which one would you like to hear today?"

"If you don't mind," Angel said, his fingertips touching, his hands working together like a spider walking on a mirror; "I'd like to hear the story again about Prince Ahmed and the Fairy Peri-Banu."

"Ah," she replied, "a very good story, indeed."

"The part about the market when Prince Husayn finds the rug."

"You mean the magic carpet?"

"The one and the same," Angel chimed back as he pulled the lap robe tight around his arms and legs in anticipation.

Martha could spin a story from a mote of dust and keep Angel occupied for hours with tales of wild Indians, pirates, gypsy princesses, wizards and dragons. Mrs. Crittenden, on the other hand, was not very good at telling stories, and by the end of the first few days of their passage she'd run through every fairy story she'd ever read or imagined. Once she ran out, she started telling Angel stories from the book she had brought with her: *Tales from the Arabian Nights.*

The Arabian tales were filled with handsome princes and magic, but there were also some rather naughty passages. It was a good book for dreaming, but not one Horace would have approved of her reading. In fact, when she got it from the booksellers in Boston she had secretly carried it home and hid it in the back of her closet until she was alone and could pack it in her suitcase without her husband knowing what she'd bought.

The stories were full of magic and excitement. She was careful, when she told the stories to Angel, to leave out the parts he shouldn't hear, like how Aladdin had the genie throw the prince into his closet every night in order to keep him from consummating his marriage with Lady Badr al-Budar.

When she had finished with Aladdin's tale, she moved on to the story of Prince Ahmad and the Fairy Peri-Banu. Even though this story seemed innocent enough, she knew she shouldn't read it to Angel. If she had any question at all regarding whether Horace would approve of her reading these far-fetched tales, she knew for certain he would not approve of Angel hearing them.

They were filled with fantasy and fancy and were not at all fit for a child. But retelling him the stories of the Arabian Nights was easier than making up stories on her own. Besides, once she had started, Angel wouldn't let her stop. So, each night she would read ahead, careful to reconstruct the story in her mind so she could retell it to Angel the next morning.

"Well," she started, "Prince Husayn went to the market one day to search for a gift for the Princess Nur al-Nihar in the hopes he might win her for his bride."

"Read it to me," Angel said, twisting a little impatiently in his chair, "I want you to read it so I can hear them talking. I know you have the book with you. I felt it in your bag when we were walking on the deck. Please read it to me. I want to see them."

"Don't worry, I'll tell you everything they say," she replied.

"I want to hear them talking," he insisted.

"I'll tell you everything," she said laughing, hoping to turn his mind away from his desire to have her read rather than just tell the story. "Well," she started again in her cheeriest storytelling voice. "The prince went to the market to find a gift for the princess."

"I said read," he demanded.

"The telling is good enough," she replied curtly.

Much to her surprise, like a brittle match struck against kindling, Angel's temper flared up angrily in response.

"You're just like father. You think I'm stupid because I'm blind. I'm not stupid. It's not the same when you tell the story. I hear it in your voice. I know it's not the same. I want to hear their words, their voices. I want to see the story in my head. I don't want to see you," he screamed, "I want to see them!"

Angel covered his face with his hands and pushed the flat of his palms deep against the sockets of his eyes. He began to rock angrily back and forth in his chair.

"The stories are so long," she said reaching out to him.

"Don't you understand," he cried, his voice jagged and wounded, "I have nothing else to see."

A porter approached them. Mrs. Crittenden turned her head for a moment as though Angel was not with her or she with him.

"Nothing…nothing else," Angel shrieked.

"Do you need something?" the porter asked, coming up alongside Angel's chair.

"No," Mrs. Crittenden said, putting her hand on Angel's leg, "he's tired is all. We're fine. Perhaps some tea would be nice?"

"Of course," he said, nodding in Angel's direction as though he was deaf and dumb as well as blind, "or some cocoa? Would the young man like cocoa?"

Angel continued to rock with his hands pressed onto his face.

"Cocoa would be lovely," Mrs. Crittenden smiled. "Thank you."

After the porter left she sat very still for a long time just watching Angel rock with his hands cradling his head like a desperately tired child. She knew she should comfort him, but she didn't say or do anything. She knew he was right. He only had what they gave him.

"There is a young woman," she said quietly, her hand reaching out to touch Angel's hand in an attempt to uncover his face and to free his eyes, "her name is Sharhrazad. She is the one who tells the stories in the book."

"Is she beautiful?"

"She is the bride of Shahyrar, King of India, and every night she weaves another tale in order to entertain the king. You see the king is angry because his first wife betrayed him, and he has vowed to marry then kill every beautiful woman he can find in order to avenge this betrayal."

"Will he kill Sharhrazad?"

"I do not believe so because he likes her stories."

"And her voice?"

"It's soft and very careful. She tells the king all she knows and sees. Each adventure she tells must be long enough to last through the night. In the morning, when the king is satisfied, he gives Sharhrazad another day to live and she rests."

"The stories are the 1001 nights he lets her live?"

"Yes."

"Where is the story now?"

"Prince Husayn is dressed like a merchant and he has traveled to the marketplace. A rug dealer is trying to sell him a carpet for thirty thousand gold pieces."

"Is that a lot?"

"Yes."

"Read."

"I will, but you must be patient. It is the end of the six hundred and forty-fifth night."

"Please," Angel begged.

Mrs. Crittenden looked first at her son's tear-streaked face, then down at the open book on her lap.

"Sharhrazad is speaking," she said slowly, letting her eyes drift ahead a moment to the story before them, "I have heard, O auspicious king, that the prince marveled with excessive marvel at the price, and, beckoning the dealer, examined his wares right well; then said he, 'A carpet such as this is selleth for a few silverlings. What special virtue hath it that thou demand therefore the sum of thirty thousand gold coins?'"

"She makes it exciting," Angel said, turning his head so his face was free again and the wind could blow against it.

"Yes," said his mother, "very exciting."

That night after he went to bed she stayed up reading ahead, carefully marking out the passages she thought Angel shouldn't hear. The next afternoon, once they had explored the ship again and settled into their deck chairs, she took out the book and read to him what she had read the night before, stopping here and there to marvel at the magic the stories wove.

"What do you think it would feel like?" he asked when she had finished reading.

"What?" she asked.

"The carpet as it moved? Do you think it bucked up like a wild horse when it took off or just rose smoothly from the ground as if someone were carrying a baby from place to place?"

"Smooth, I would think," she said, closing her own eyes in order to try and imagine the thrill of being on a flying carpet.

"Do you think it's cold?"

"The carpet?"

"The air. Is it like this, with the wind blowing cold against your face? Or is it warm like being on a beach?"

"Warm, I should think."

"Yes," he said, his eyes flickering from side to side as if he could see the heat of the sun shimmering on the curled surface of the flying carpet, "I believe you're right. Warm. Like you are riding above the wind and close to the sun. Read," he again commanded like one of the Sultans from the stories.

And she did.

The morning after they arrived in London the hotel bellboy came to their room with a telegram from Horace saying they were to return to Boston immediately. The message was brief. Europe was on the brink of war. Their tickets would be wired to the hotel. The boat would leave at nine that evening.

How like Horace, Mrs. Crittenden thought, to send commands rather than fond wishes by telegram. They'd hardly set foot in London and now would have to leave. The thought of having come so far and to have nothing to show for it angered her.

"Please get us packed to return," Mrs. Crittenden ordered Martha.

Mrs. Crittenden turned away from Martha in order to speak to Angel. She had no desire to see the heavy expression of anxiety flush across Martha's still sick face, "Angel and I are going out. We'll be back by supper. We'll be leaving shortly afterwards."

She took Angel's hand and they left the room. When they got to the hotel lobby she told the manager they would be departing for America after supper, and she asked him where they might buy a rug. The manager told her she should go to Akmed, a merchant he knew personally and trusted. Akmed had a shop on the other side of town. The manager offered to arrange a carriage for them. Akmed was, the manager told her, the best rug merchant in all of London.

The driver delivered them to the mouth of the alleyway and asked if he should wait.

"Yes," Mrs. Crittenden said. "This won't take long."

She took a tight angry hold of Angel's hand and headed down the narrow alleyway. She had no idea what the brink of war was or whether or not the war was happening in London that very minute. In fact, she was not altogether sure Horace wasn't making it all up in order to force her to come home.

"What's that smell?" Angel asked lifting his head and turning it from side to side the way a turtle might do when trying to locate the sun.

"Keep your eyes open," she said giving his hand a squeeze. He looked blind and vulnerable when he closed his eyes. "Coffee roasters. They must be in one of those buildings down the alleyway. To your left there's a café."

"Smells burnt," Angel said, turning his head in the direction of the smell. "Can I taste the coffee?"

"I don't think you'd like it."

"I'd like to taste it," he said, tilting his head back and letting his eyes close again.

"Open those eyes," she said, speeding up as she moved down the alleyway towards Akmed's shop.

"Why are we running?" Angel asked as they moved past the smells of the burnt roasting coffee and the busy cafés.

"Running?"

"You're pulling my arm. I can hardly keep up with you."

"We have to hurry."

"Why?"

"Because we have to go."

"Go where?"

"Your father said we have to go home."

"Are we running to the ship?"

"We're looking for a carpet."

"Like the one Husayn found?" Angel asked excitedly.

"Yes. But we have to hurry."

Ever since she read about the magic flying carpet she had a strong urge to buy a rug. She had fretted about how she would explain this rug to Horace, but his telegram this morning helped her understand the rug for what it was: a way for Angel to have the world. If she could find a beautiful rug then all Angel would have to do would be to sit upon it and it wouldn't matter one whit that they didn't get to go to Venice or Rome or Egypt. They would never be stuck in Boston again. She would read the world to him, yes, that's precisely what she'd do. She would open his world with books and take him anywhere he wanted to go: India, Africa, Rome, Greece, Paris, and even the frozen seas of Antarctica. The rug would be like new eyes for him.

"Here it is," she said, seeing the doorway of the store. It was just as the hotel manager had described it, a small opened door with a long rug spilling out from it into the alleyway.

"Come in," the bandy-legged merchant called as they approached.

"I'm looking for a Mr. Akmed," Mrs. Crittenden announced stiffly.

"I am the same," Akmed said as though he had just been called to receive a great prize.

"I'm looking for a rug."

"I have rugs," he said smiling, his hand sweeping through the air into the waiting opened door. "What rug do you desire?"

"Like the one Prince Husayn found," Angel offered.

"Ah, yes, the magic carpet!"

"You know about it?" Angel asked.

"Every rug merchant knows of Prince Husayn and his magic carpet."

"You have it?"

"I have many rugs, but not that rug. If I had that rug I would not be here in a dark alleyway in London. I would be a rich man flying around the world. I would be the king!"

34

"Oh," said Angel disappointedly.

"Do not be disappointed. There are other kinds of magic carpets here," announced the merchant. He looked at Mrs. Crittenden and extended his hand to Angel as if to say he saw the boy was blind and wanted her permission to take him into the store. She nodded her head and Mr. Akmed took Angel by the hand.

"Let's see what we can find."

Although the doorway was narrow, the store was deep and wide inside and stacked with rugs from floor to ceiling. Akmed snapped his fingers and an assistant came into view.

"This fine young man is looking for a magic carpet," Akmed announced.

"Yes," his assistant answered.

The assistant scurried like a little gray rat from pile to pile pulling a small rug here, another there, and placing them in the center of the room. When he had assembled ten or twelve of them Akmed nodded his head and the assistant began unfurling them, one by one and laying them out on the floor as though he had been told to create a crazy quilt with them.

"The first magic carpets," Akmed explained, waving his hands across the spread of carpets before him, "were as big as a small village. Two, maybe three hundred mounted soldiers could be carried on them. They were used for war. They are part of the magic of the Kabbalah. But that is not the kind of carpet you are looking for, heh?"

Angel turned toward his mother.

"No," she answered for him, "not one so big. Certainly not one for war."

"We have enough of war today, heh? Let us get back to more pleasant things, but first, a question," Akmed said, shaking his head in disbelief. "A handsome man-child such as this. He cannot speak for himself?"

"I can speak," Angel answered, his head upright, his eyes

wide open.

"The carpet is for you, yes?"

"Yes."

"You must speak up. How big should this carpet be? What kind of magic are you looking for?"

"Not so big as a village, and nothing for war."

"What kind of carpet do you dream of?"

"One that could fly!"

Akmed tugged at the longest hair in his beard.

"To fly could be dangerous in these times. But, as I said, there are other kinds of magic. Take this one, for instance."

Akmed stooped to pick up the edge of a large Ushak carpet adorned with two central star-like medallions.

"It is very beautiful and very old. Touch it."

Angel let his hand run against the short silky grain of the rug.

"Smell it," he said, holding the carpet up to Angel's face. "What do you smell?"

Mrs. Crittenden inched forward into the center of the room. She wanted to touch and smell the rugs as well. Mr. Akmed looked at her and shook his head. She understood and stayed just at the edge and watched.

"It smells of animals."

"Yes, of animals. Of the sheep that gave their wool, the camel that carried it on its back, and the king's dogs that slept on it in front of the hearth."

"A king owned this rug?" Angel gasped in disbelief.

"He owned many rugs. His palace was full of rugs and riches. He was once good. He turned bad with greed and resentment. When he did, he lost everything, including this rug."

"You have the king's rug?"

"Eventually all the best rugs come to me."

"And mine?"

"This, I believe, must be yours," Akmed said. Putting down the Ushak, he walked over to a modest rectangular deep red

Turkoman rug. It was Ashoan's rug. It had grown dusty from the trip and from sitting in Akmed's London shop for the last four years, but it was still beautiful. Angel held his breath.

"I believe this is yours," Akmed said, smoothing the little rug with admiration. "The likes of it will not come this way again."

Mrs. Crittenden could see there were other more colorful rugs on the floor than the one Akmed had picked for Angel, but before she could cry out to tell him to consider the Ushak or the stunning gold, blue and red Egyptian Mameluke medallion carpet, Angel had touched the careful tight weave of Ashoan's wedding rug.

"Ohhhh," Angel crooned, "the stitches are so small and tight. This rug could keep the cold out."

"You are a very bright young man. This carpet bears a cross, a hatchlu, marking it as the flap on a tent door."

"What colors?"

"Breathe in its smell. Taste the black smoke of the campfire and the warm golden sand of the desert. Feel the heat of the sun as it kisses the earth each evening as it sets warm and red along the horizon. These are the colors of your rug."

Angel brushed the nap of the rug with the back of his hand. He held the rug up to his face.

"Yes," he said, "and the design?"

"There are two strong rows of birds, their wings flapping on either side, a band of flowers across the top and four groves of trees growing in each quadrant of the hatchlu. There are also camels and cross-hatched symbols so common we have carelessly lost their meaning."

"These are the flowers?" Angel asked, his hand resting on the small patch of flowers at the top of the hatchlu.

"Precisely."

"Umm," Angel hummed quietly as his fingers explored the stitched edges of the rug, "and the magic?"

"Ah yes, the magic. It is there for you to find."

"Mother?" Angel called as he moved his head from side to side, holding the rug out in front of him in an attempt to locate her in the dark room.

"Yes, Angel."

"Could I have this one?"

Mrs. Crittenden looked at the rug Angel wanted. She took one step forward, careful in her step not to put her foot on any of the rugs spread before her. She thought the others might be more beautiful, but she could see in the way Angel held the little rug that it was the right one for him.

"How much?" she asked Akmed.

Akmed thought for a moment, twisted the thin tip of his beard in his fingers and looked hard at his assistant as if to signal him to keep quiet.

"Ten pounds."

The assistant let out a low whistling hiss against his sharp front teeth. He stooped down and began to fold and roll each of the remaining rugs in order to tuck them back into their rightful piles.

Mrs. Crittenden wasn't any good at math and had no idea if ten pounds was ten dollars or ten hundred dollars.

"Ten," she said, counting out the strange English bills from her purse and offering them to Akmed. "Is it a good rug?" she asked, knowing she would have to make a full report of the value of her purchase to Horace when she got home.

"One of my best. Made by a young Turkoman bride as part of her dowry."

"Like Sharhrazad," mused Angel.

"May Allah bless you and may the rug bring you pleasure," Akmed said, bowing deeply as he took the money. He carefully folded the rug, rolled it tightly and bound it with a piece of string before he handed it to Angel. Angel thanked the merchant, bowing slightly as he did so. Gift in hand, he and his mother left Akmed's little shop.

The assistant waited until Mrs. Crittenden and Angel's footsteps had fallen silent in the alleyway.

"Ten?" he scowled, once he was sure they were gone.

"Yes," Akmed shot back, folding his arms in front of him.

"It's worth every penny of twenty and you could have gotten thirty or forty from someone so foolish as this mother. She had no idea what she was buying."

"Did you not see the child was blind? Any more than ten for a blind child would have blackened the magic."

"Magic!" the assistant scoffed. "Since when do you believe in anything more magic than two coins rubbing against each other? When the war comes charging down our alleyway, how many rich Americans do you think will find their way to your shop? Your wife should spit in your food tonight for starving her children."

"Enough!" Akmed shouted, clapping his hands together like an angry genie calling forth spirits to do his bidding. Spinning around on his small slippered feet, he disappeared into the alleyway.

The ship pulled away from the port into the endless ocean filled night. As soon as the boat was free of the dock most of the worried passengers moved quietly to their cabins.

The ship had been nearly fully booked, so the three of them, Mrs. Crittenden, Angel and Martha, had to take what they could get and were sharing a large cabin instead of a suite. Horace had made no apologies in his telegram for the inconvenience of the booking. Mrs. Crittenden instructed Martha to take the small bed on the right and told Angel he would have to make do with the couch.

"I'll put the rug here," Angel said, struggling to untie the rough twine with which Akmed had bound it.

"I'll do that," Mrs. Crittenden said, freeing the rug and rolling it out before him in front of his couch.

"Let me see it," he said, his eyes widening as the glory of the little rug unrolled at his feet. "The flowers are here, yes?"

"Yes."

"And the camels here and the beating wings, here, right?"

Angel's hands moved quickly from place to place on the rug. He closed his eyes for a minute as if he were memorizing every stitch of the precious rug.

"Yes."

Martha had put out fresh nightclothes for Mrs. Crittenden and Angel. Afterwards, she excused herself and pulled the curtain around her bed in order to change into her own gown and robe. Mrs. Crittenden and Angel could hear her crying.

"Will it take us as long to get home as it did to get here?" Angel asked as he turned his head towards the curtains of Martha's bed.

His eyes were opened wide and he looked in his mother's direction as if to say, listen, Mother, Martha is crying because she is afraid she is going to be sick again or worse, that she is going to die either at the hands of the war or the sea before they could ever get back to Boston again.

"It is the same distance in one direction as it is in the other," Mrs. Crittenden said wearily and a little annoyed.

"But the crossing will be smoother? Right?" Angel said, his voice rising slightly. "The wind is with us on the return, isn't it?"

Mrs. Crittenden looked from Angel to the curtains drawn tightly around Martha's bed. She knew Angel was right: Martha was afraid. She worried Angel might also be afraid of not only the crossing, but of the war.

"Yes, smoother," she replied, hoping to calm them both.

Martha quit crying.

As Martha's crying ceased, Mrs. Crittenden realized her own disappointment at having to return to the dull gray streets of Boston and to Horace.

"And you are right, my little Angel," she said, her voice

softening a touch in shame, "the wind is with us on the return."

"And you'll read to us? To Martha and me, to make the night go faster?"

Martha pulled the edge of the curtain back so she could see Angel and his mother.

"What do you think, Martha?" Mrs. Crittenden asked as she slipped off her shoes and began to rub her toes against the silken grain of the red rug. Alone by itself in their tiny cabin, the rug seemed bigger: warm and inviting, even beautiful. The crowded dark interior of Akmed's shop had not done it justice.

"It would help me sleep," Martha said honestly.

"Tell her about Sharhrazad," Angel prompted, his eyes flickering from Martha to his mother then back down to the rows of flying geese on his beautiful new carpet.

"She was a princess," Mrs. Crittenden began.

"A beautiful princess," Angel added, "and she was married to a sad king who had been hurt and wanted to kill all the beautiful women in the world. But Sharhrazad was clever and told him stories every night to make him forget his hurt. And because he liked the stories he didn't kill her. The stories kept both of them alive."

"How long?" Martha asked.

"For a thousand and one nights," Angel crowed, his arms flung wide as though he could catch the whole world in his outstretched hands.

"Sharhrazad is speaking," Mrs. Crittenden began as she opened her book and drifted down onto the small red carpet to read. "Then she said, it is the end of the six-hundredth and sixtieth night," and as Mrs. Crittenden read, she believed she could feel the carpet she was sitting on shift a bit beneath her, carrying them beyond the night, the war, the rocking ship, and the cold dark blue of the sea.

As his mother began to read, Angel drew the soft wool blanket of his bed around his shoulders. Martha came to sit next to him, her face calm for the moment, calm and sure the passage would be swifter and the wind would be with them.

As the words of Sharhrazad came to life in the room Mrs. Crittenden felt a peace come to her heart. When her hand brushed against the fine silken grain of the rug her anger at Horace for making them return to dull and dreary Boston melted as though the rug was, indeed, magic.

As she read, letting her hand play against the smooth sweet surface of the rug beneath her, her life was lifted up and she felt as though the moment they were living would last forever.

CHAPTER 4

1915
THE RECTOR

"Lead a good long life," the rector announced, his right arm gesturing in the air as though there was an anxious congregation gathered at his feet, "or should I say a long good life? Yes, that's it. Live a long good life, and you get a good long funeral."

"Sir," Mildred, his housekeeper, said as she came into the room. She was carrying a silver tray with a generous glass of sherry and an uncorked bottle. She set the tray down on the little table by the rector's reading chair, and walked to the window to pull the draperies closed.

"Ashes to ashes," he mused, "dust to dust. So really simple isn't it? Pure poetry."

"I suppose you could think of it that way."

"Lead a sweet short life," he added lifting his glass, "you get a short sweet funeral." He emptied the glass and quickly poured another.

"The little blind boy?" Mildred asked.

"Angel. Aptly named, don't you think? Angel Crittenden. Blind since birth and dead on the eve of his thirteenth birthday. Hardly a life."

"He was a nice boy."

"I christened him."

"I remember," Mildred offered. "His mother seemed in such a hurry to have him named. Like she thought he might not be with her long. If I remember correctly, the father was away..."

"On business. A very busy man. But he made it to the funeral. Even the most distant of relatives make it to the funeral," the rector added, taking up the second glass of sherry.

"Ah, yes. Will there be anything else, Father?"

"I never understand why they come."

"Comfort's what most people want, Father."

The rector finished the second glass and poured a third a little slower than he had poured the second.

"I thought it would be comforting to say he was a special child of God."

"Ah, he was. Those strange blind eyes...always dancing around like he *could* see everything there was in the world, both living and gone. It was a little eerie."

"That he came to us as a gift..."

"Children are a gift all right."

"Do you believe in ghosts, Mildred?"

"Ghosts, Father?"

"Not the ones floating around in sheets and scaring people, but spirits. Ghosts. Pieces of ourselves that get caught in this world and can't leave."

"Can't say I've ever seen one," Mildred said, gathering her skirt tightly around her legs and twisting a little from side to side in order to look over her shoulder and survey the darkened room.

"I've felt them. Children mostly. It's like they stay back a little to see what we're going to say about them and how we're going to grieve them being gone."

"Easy to imagine a child doing such a thing. Would you like anything else?"

The rector drank the third glass. He didn't bother taking time to savor its sweetness before he poured a scant fourth. He shifted a little in his chair, picked up the glass and put it down again.

"He was in the chapel today," he said, picking up the glass again.

"Blessed Mary," Mildred said, crossing herself and quickly kissing her hand. "You can trust me," she said, drawing up close to the rector and sitting easy like a child by his feet.

The rector waited until Mildred was quiet and settled before he spoke again.

"It was like he really was an angel," the rector began tentatively, his cheeks flushed with the warmth of the quickly drunk sherry. "There was a light flitting about the chapel. It had a hum in it. A noise you had to strain to hear. Like it had a breath you could feel against your face. Mildred," the rector's hands were shaking as he held them up for her to see, "it was as real as the prayer book I was holding in my hands."

"Dear Jesus," Mildred whispered. Looking around the room, she crossed herself again.

"The light was dancing around the chapel, swooping this way and that. I had planned to read the service from the prayer book, short and sweet like Angel's life."

"Always liked the prayer book service," Mildred said, knowing there wasn't much you could say when a child died.

"The mother took comfort in my words and quit crying. And when she did, the light seemed to settle."

"Heard tell he died of pneumonia."

"The mother had gone home for the night to get some rest. The father had stayed at the hospital. When I got to the hospital the father was holding Angel in his lap like he was a baby. Angel filled his father's arms, his long skinny legs dangling almost to the floor. When I stepped into the room the father was just sitting there, still as a marble statue, not rocking or singing or talking. The father had his face pressed up against the boy's fevered head. The doctor had called and said I should come to do the Holy Unction."

The rector picked up the glass again and took another sip.

"The light, the one I saw in the chapel at the funeral, settled on the father's face."

"Ahh," Mildred drew a quick frightened breath. "Not the mother's? I heard the father was a bad one."

"He looked transformed."

"Transformed?" Mildred's voice sounded alarmed.

The rector took the last of the sherry in the bottom of his glass in one swallow. He considered pouring another but thought better of it.

"It made me angry," the priest said, picking up the bottle in haste to pour himself another anyway.

"Angry?" Mildred said, a little frightened.

"I wanted the light to fall on me, not on him. The father was never there for that little boy. Never. Wouldn't even give his son his name. I was the one who came to the hospital to hold Angel when he was first born. I was the one who christened him. I was there for him. I sat by his bedside and prayed. I heard his confessions. I gave him the Holy Unction."

"Yes," Mildred said, not fully understanding what he was saying, but wanting to give him support, "you were there for him. Everyone knows you were there for that little boy."

The priest finished his drink, and as he did, he drew in a long deep breath.

"What's a fool priest like me doing talking about ghosts? There's just one ghost, the Holy Ghost, isn't that right, Mildred?"

"Only ghost in these parts I know about," she said getting up from the floor.

"It was nothing really," he said, setting his empty glass on the tray, "just the late afternoon light playing tricks on me. Boston in winter can make you pretty daft."

He picked up the cork on the tray and tapped it into the bottle and waved his hand over the tray as though he was a magician and could make everything disappear: the tray, the empty glass, the dark of the room, the memory of the light dancing in the chapel, the vision of Angel dying in his father's arms.

"Mrs. Crittenden's man came by with a package for you after the funeral," Mildred said as she picked up the tray.

"For me?"

"Yes, he said Mrs. Crittenden wanted you to have it. I put it over there on the floor near your desk. Odd package, a bit long and on the thin side, but heavy. Need anything else?"

"No, and Mildred," the rector said raising his finger to his lips.

"Not a word," she said, "you can trust me."

"Thank you," he said, and turned away from her.

When Mildred left, the rector walked over to the package on the floor by his desk. It was wrapped in an old sheet and was about four feet long. Mildred had been right, it was a little heavy, but not so heavy he couldn't easily carry it, just heavy enough to make it a bit awkward.

He took the package to his chair and unwrapped it. Inside he found a deep red rug and a note from Mrs. Crittenden. The rug looked to be foreign. The rector had seen many rugs of its type in homes of his wealthier parishioners. It was beautiful in a dark and subtle way. The light seemed to dance across the fine fibers of its surface. It looked to be rather new, but most of the fringe had been worn off or pulled out as though someone had nervously twisted it off. The note was handwritten on Mrs. Crittenden's personal stationary.

Dear Father:

Angel took such comfort in your prayers for him. He said he could feel your words lifting him up. I believe Angel would like you to have this. It was one of his favorite possessions. I cannot bear to have it near me now that he's gone.

Sincerely,

Mrs. Horace Crittenden II

The rector rubbed his hand against the smooth grain of the rug. The room was cold, but the rug felt warm as though it had been sitting by the fireplace or perhaps someone had recently been sleeping on it.

"Heavenly Father," he whispered under his breath. As his hand moved across the tight pattern of the rug he thought he could see the figure of Angel rolling across it, pulling at the fringe in order to fold the rug back onto himself as though he were playing a game of hide and seek. The rector swore he could hear the boy laughing.

"Angel?" the rector gasped. He looked around the darkened room for a flicker of light. "I prayed for you, remember?"

He kept searching the room while his hand continued to play against the rug.

"*A gift!*" the boy's ghostly laughter chimed.

The rector's hands trembled a little.

"They were words to comfort your parents. You were a gift," he said.

"*A gift.*" Like a cough or an echo, the sound clattered through the room.

"I didn't know what else to do. All I have are words."

With that, the room turned cold as though a window had blown open or the fire gone out.

The rector slid from his chair to the small rug on the floor. He carefully placed his hands on the two patches where Ashoan had woven the flowers in the corners to comfort her. He put his forehead on the mihrab in the small space in between.

"What could I have done or said that would have changed things?" he cried into the dusty countenance of the rug, hoping Angel would hear him.

He pulled his knees up tight against his chest. His breathing slowed as he tried to calm himself. Even if he still could, he knew he would not cry. It had been years since he had let his despair with God and his impotence as a priest escape in such a shameful way.

"I need your gift. Touch me with your light," he whispered to Angel, his eyes shut tight. "Let me be transformed."

The rug was warm beneath his hands. The room was still.

"Why did you touch him," he asked the empty room, "and not me?"

No answer came.

"Let me be transformed," he prayed.

"Sweet Angel of God," he called out so fiercely his body rocked from side to side and his fingers became entangled in the few remaining bits of twisted fringe. He pulled the rug over himself and breathed in the dust from the rug. His heart raced with the wild odor of wool and sweat and his own alcohol-soaked breath.

"I will do anything, anything you say," he begged the now empty room, "just let me be transformed."

And then he wept.

CHAPTER 5

1954
THE HOUSEKEEPER

The first time Mildred found the rector prostrate on the rug, she rushed into the room thinking he might have taken a fit.

"Father," she cried, "are you okay?"

The rector didn't stir.

"Father," she called out again, moving closer this time, afraid to touch him lest he be dead.

He raised his head and pushed himself up slowly with his hands until the weight of his body rested on his heels.

"I didn't mean to scare you," he said.

"Did you fall?"

"No."

Mildred did not know what to say. The way the rector was crouched over the rug made him seem more animal than man. It frightened her.

"I was praying," he said, rising up from the floor. His slippers were at the edge of the rug and he casually slid his feet into them.

"On the rug?"

"It's a prayer rug."

"I've heard of magic rugs, but don't think I've ever heard of anyone praying to a rug."

"I'm not praying to the rug, just using the rug to pray on. Lots of people around the world pray on rugs."

Mildred had never heard of such a thing, but she wasn't one to challenge the rector. She was quite sure praying on a rug wasn't a Christian thing.

"Do you think the little boy prayed on the rug?" she asked. She recognized the rug as the one Mrs. Crittenden had given to the rector after Angel died.

"Probably not."

The rector folded his hands. Mildred waited for him to speak.

"There's no need to worry," he told Mildred, stepping away from the rug. "The Bible says you should pray in your closet, but you see, I don't have a closet, so I pray on this rug. It's private."

"I won't tell anyone."

"I know I can trust you."

It was nearly four o'clock.

"Would you like me to bring you your sherry?"

"Yes," the rector replied, and he walked slowly to his study and sat down at his desk to wait for her to bring his afternoon aperitif.

That was the last time they ever spoke about the rug, but not the last time Mildred found him kneeling on it and praying.

"He was an odd duck, he was," she told the lawyer.

Mildred had been housekeeper to the rector for nearly forty-five years when he died. Forty-five years of hiding the hundreds of empty sherry bottles. Forty-five years of keeping his crazy secrets about seeing ghosts and praying on his little rug.

"Hmmm," the lawyer said, looking over the top edge of his glasses as though he was not at all interested in what Mildred had to say and, frankly, didn't care.

"Took his sherry quite seriously," she offered, feeling a need to at last confess and get it off her chest. When the rector was alive, she'd had to keep her confessions down to the usual bad thoughts and occasional swear word. For forty-five years, she'd kept his secrets bottled up inside because there was no one she could rightly tell.

"Four o'clock, every afternoon on the dot. I'd carry the tray to his study and he'd make this show of pouring a small glass. He'd sip it slow, just a wee taste like it was some kind of medicine his doctor had prescribed to settle his stomach or help with his appetite. Didn't have any trouble with the appetite either, if you want to know the truth. Liked his sweets too.

"Sometimes he'd cork the bottle after he poured that first glass. Never filled his glass to the top, and never left the cork in for long, if you know what I mean. Had to hide the empty bottles. There were so many of them, especially after he started seeing ghosts. Had to take the bottles home in my bag. Couldn't put them in the parish trash. No, that wouldn't do. People would talk for sure."

The lawyer cleared his throat.

"I need to see some identification," he said.

"James Allen Whitley. I have known you since you were ten and singing in the children's choir for Mass on Sunday morning and causing mischief, if you don't mind my saying. Good thing you became a lawyer, because you weren't much of a choirboy if you ask me. And, if you need some kind of proof I'm who I say I am, then shame on both you and your mother."

"I know who you are, but the law requires I see some identification of the parties involved before I can read the will. Can you show me your driver's license?"

"Don't have one."

"A passport?"

"Now, what on God's good earth would I need with a passport? Haven't been anywhere in my life but this end of Boston. Last time I looked, you didn't need a passport to cross the street in Boston. Am I right?"

"Anything with your name on it?"

Mildred reached into her purse and pulled out the letter she'd gotten from James Allen Whitley's office about the reading of the rector's will.

"Just this letter you sent me," she said, putting the letter on his desk and sliding it towards him so he could see her name on the envelope.

"Shall we proceed?" James Whitley pushed his glasses up and opened the folder containing the will.

"Sometimes, when he had a glass or two, he'd start telling me things...crazy things like seeing ghosts."

"I don't believe—"

Mildred interrupted him.

"First one was when that little boy, Angel, died. There were others afterwards. Too many to count, if you ask me. He'd see them and, don't you know, he'd be crouched down on that rug of his, praying. He had this rug he kept in his bedroom. It was one of those secrets he asked me to keep."

"I think secrets are best kept..."

"Called it a prayer rug. Never heard of such a thing in my life. But, the rector talked about it like it was something everyone should have. Don't know anybody but the rector who had one. Didn't seem Christian to me. But, whenever he'd see some ghost or drink one too many glasses of sherry, down he'd go, and I'd find him praying on that rug. Always scared me, made me think he was having some kind of seizure or maybe one of them episodes where you lose a little bit of your mind. First time I saw him crouched on that rug like he was searching for something, I thought he was dead. Dead..."

"I need to read the will..."

"I was the one who found him."

Mildred grabbed her letter off the lawyer's desk and stuffed it into her purse. She crossed herself before going on, "God have mercy on his soul."

"I'm sure He will."

"Not so sure myself, the rector seeing ghosts all the time and praying on that rug. Used to say the ghost of that little boy, Angel, was haunting him. Sounded like the work of the Devil, if you ask me."

"You're here today so I can read you the will..."

"Carried that rug out to the back stoop once a week and hung it on the line so I could beat it with my broom. Worried sometimes that if I beat it too hard the Devil might jump right out of it and grab me. Used to scare me to death to touch it."

"Let's begin…" James Allen pushed his glasses back up onto his nose and took up the rector's Last Will and Testament.

Mildred clicked the latch of her purse shut, squared her shoulders and sat up as tall and as straight as she could. She was slightly stooped from picking up after the rector all those long years.

"Took good care of him for near forty-five years…never missed a day."

"To my kind and faithful servant, Mildred," James Allen began.

Mildred took in a deep breath and closed her eyes.

"I leave my rug."

Mildred's eyes snapped open. She thought she felt the faint laughter of a child brush against her ear.

"What did you say?" she demanded, her eyes searching the room, half scared she'd see the ghost of Angel.

"The rector, in his will, said he left you his rug."

"Which rug?"

"How many rugs did he own?"

"Wasn't but one rug I know about."

"I guess that's the one."

"Don't want it."

"But it's yours now."

"You can keep it."

Mildred leaned forward in her chair.

"Did he leave me anything else?"

"Just the rug."

"I'll be going."

Mildred stood up and walked to the door.

"Aren't you going to take the rug?" James Allen asked.

The rug was rolled up in a tight bundle on the floor in the corner of his office.

"No, sir. Got no use for it. It's yours."

"But, I can't keep it."

"Then I'd advise you to give it away as quickly as you can. There's something unnatural about that rug. Been beating it for near forty years, and I know for certain the Devil's still in it."

James Allen sat at his desk watching the last bit of afternoon light move across the floor of his office. He felt a chill pass over him like a shadow.

The rug was rolled up in a bundle in the corner of the room. He'd been afraid to either leave the room or touch the rug ever since Mildred had left more than two hours ago.

He couldn't keep the rug. It wasn't his to keep and he wasn't quite sure it was his to give away.

He looked at his watch. It was four o'clock. If he hurried, he could take the rug to the antique dealer on High Street and get rid of it.

A sudden violent whoosh of wind rattled the windows of his office and made a high whistling sound almost like the cry of a small child.

"My rug..."

"Who's that? What?" James Allen called out.

The room was still and quiet.

James Allen pulled on his overcoat and put on his gloves. He picked up the little rug and ran.

CHAPTER 6

1967
THE TEACHER

Mary Frances carefully laid the pretty rectangular rug in the middle of the living room floor. She smoothed the tattered edges of the carpet with the broad flat palms of her hands. She took a single straight-backed wooden chair from the dining room, placed it at the top edge of the rug and draped the seat of the chair with a freshly ironed white linen tablecloth as if it were an altar. She hummed while she worked.

"Room for the Holy Ghost," she chanted high up in her head, imitating Sister Agnes James, the fat mean-eyed nun who taught geography and women's health in Saint Ignatius High School when Mary Frances was a student there forty years ago.

Sister Agnes James took great pleasure in advising the young women in her health class on the pressing need to always leave room for the Holy Ghost when they danced with the boys after the basketball games. Whenever she talked about the Holy Ghost, her eyes would narrow and she'd start to creep down the aisles of the desks with a strange stalking motion. This, together with the odd notion of the Holy Ghost being interested in slipping between groping adolescent dancing partners in the school gymnasium, sent most of the Women's Health students into uncontrolled fits of laughter. Sister Agnes James silenced these outbursts with a violent slash of her yardstick across the top of her desk.

Mary Frances did not laugh. One Friday evening while she and Jimmy Jenkins were dancing to the intoxicating sound of Irving Berlin's "Blue Skies" Jimmy was singing along and his lips brushed lightly against Mary Frances' cheek. At the same moment his lips touched her face, he pulled her waist closer to his. Before Mary Frances could either bend to Jimmy's desires or push him away, Sister Agnes James' fat fist angrily wedged a place between her and Jimmy Jenkins, calling forth the power of the Holy Ghost.

Much to her horror, in the split second before she could jump back, Mary Frances felt something stiff and hard in Jimmy's pants. She ran from the gym. It was the last time she ever danced with a boy.

Mary Frances gave a quick glance over the room and her handiwork, closed her eyes tightly and let out a quick sharp command, "Go away. Enough!"

Mary Frances had forty years of experience dealing with the nagging voice of Sister Agnes James in her head and knew she had better shut it out completely if she expected to succeed with her plan.

Her plan was to beckon the ghost of Flannery O'Connor. Mary Frances was quite certain the rug would help her do it. Ever since she had found the wonderful red rug at the antique shop on High Street in Boston last summer, things had begun to happen.

For one, she no longer seemed to care that her students at St. Mary's School rolled their eyes when she talked about the fine texture of a short story or the hypnotizing rhythm of language. In truth, she was beginning not to care at all about what anyone thought about her. Having the rug in her house made her feel she had at last found a part of herself she had lost long ago. She felt bold and new. In fact, when a certain Tiffany Johnson strolled into class ten minutes late the day before, rather than look the other way or write her down as late in her grade book, Mary Frances had stopped her lecture just long enough to mention she'd be glad to pray for Tiffany's punctuality. The comment drew a ripple of laughter, but since she didn't budge or flinch, the laughter soon turned a serious corner. Unlike Sister Agnes James, Mary Francis didn't need to slap a ruler on a desk to make her class get quiet.

When she bought the rug and brought it into her home, she began hearing voices. There was Sister Agnes James' voice, coming in loud and clear as usual, joined by others, including her dead mother's and grandmother's. Two days after the rug came into her house she woke up at four o'clock in the morning to the sweet smell of her long-ago-departed father's pipe tobacco filling her bedroom. All in all, it had been quite exciting.

Although she had not yet seen a ghost, she knew she was not afraid to encounter one. In fact, she was secretly delighted at the prospect of some night catching her father walking through her room.

She had less of a desire to see the ghosts of her mother and grandmother, but would admit she had enjoyed hearing their soft meddling voices as they wove themselves in and out of her consciousness. The now nearly constant nagging chatter of Sister Helen was beginning to get on her nerves. But, even that turned out to be a good thing, because that's how she discovered the secret power of the rug.

One day, when the voice of Sister Agnes James was pestering her about the virtues of cleanliness, pure thoughts, sacrifice, and daily prayer, Mary Frances decided to clean the house in order to shut the nun out. She took all the books off the shelf in the living room and wiped them down with vinegar water. She emptied the china hutch and washed her mother's collection of china teacups and her grandmother's Hummel figurines.

Unfortunately, even after she had finished those tasks, the nun's wretched voice was still ringing in her ears, so Mary Frances decided to wash the wooden floors in the dining room.

When she snatched up the little rug off the floor and took it to the back porch for a good shaking, much to her surprise, the voice of Sister Agnes James disappeared. It was like she had never before been in Mary France's head. As long as she shook the rug she couldn't hear one word Sister Agnes James was saying. When Mary Frances put the rug down on the floor, however, Sister Agnes James came back full throttle.

Out of frustration, Mary Frances stepped on the rug, and, just like that, Sister Agnes James disappeared again. Mary Frances cleverly moved the rug into the hallway, where she would be able to step on it every time she crossed through to the dining room or the kitchen or into her bedroom or the bath.

Having the rug was like having a volume control dial with which she could turn the voice on and off. If she timed it just right, she could pop off the nun's tirades about washing hands, leaving room for the Holy Ghost, and the naming of the seven great oceans.

The way Mary Frances had it figured, if the rug could make the nun's voice disappear without ever having asked it to do so, surely it could grant her one small wish. That's when she got the idea about Flannery O'Connor.

She was desperate, truly soul-starving desperate, for someone to talk to other than her students. The faculty not only didn't talk to her, she knew they laughed at her behind her back. They quit speaking to her years ago when she announced she believed the biggest problem the school faced was its lack of intellectual integrity. When the chairman of her department asked her to explain what she was talking about, Mary Frances said the school lacked intellectual integrity because it failed to demand the same kind of scholarship from the faculty as they demanded of their students. When pressed further, she said quite bluntly that she doubted there was even one faculty person present who had read one new book or had one new idea in the last ten years. In truth, she felt relieved to have at last said what had long been on her mind, but she was saddened by the silence that followed.

How she picked Flannery O'Connor was easy. She simply took out a piece of paper and wrote down the names of all the people she most wanted to talk to when she first arrived in heaven, and Flannery topped the list. Her mother, father, and grandmother, were on the list, of course, as well as Shakespeare and Jane Austen. She also thought she would really like to talk to Hemingway. She truly loved the sparseness of his writing, his knack for stripping away everything you didn't need to tell in order to create a story, but she really didn't expect to see him in heaven since he had committed suicide. Ditto on Sylvia Plath. Such a shame, she liked them both, despite their moral failings.

In the end, Mary Frances came to the wonderful conclusion that Flannery O'Connor was easily her top pick. Flannery's writing crackled with sparse terse language, plus she had a razor-sharp edge to her storytelling voice. Also, her characters nearly drove you crazy with their burning desires and shocking destitution. Yet, despite the stunning level of depravity in Flannery's writing, she lived a moral life, and was a devout Catholic.

The clock on the mantel struck midnight. Mary Frances checked her watch, and went to her desk in order to pick up the two pictures of Flannery O'Connor she had photocopied at the library. In one, Flannery was dressed in a fancy party dress sitting demurely with her legs crossed, looking young and pretty with a Mona Lisa kind of smile on her face. The picture had been taken at a book-signing party for *Wise Blood* at Georgia State College for Women in 1952. The other was taken ten years later on the steps of her home, Andalusia, in Milledgeville. From the change in her physical appearance between the two pictures, it was clear that by the time she had taken up residence in Andalusia, Lupus had begun to rule Flannery's life.

Mary Frances thought the first picture to be prettier, but the second to be more about the real Flannery O'Connor. It showed her standing on the steps of her family home, her slightly swollen frame cinched in a cotton dress and balanced precariously on metal crutches. One of her beloved peacocks, tail draping down the brick steps, took up residence beside her.

Mary Frances placed both pictures on the seat of the chair and arranged a peacock plume over the top of them. She had found the feather at an antique store in Cameron Village near the college. The peacock plume was one of a dozen such feathers stuffed into a chipped ceramic vase of a fan dancer. The dealer had wanted to sell the feathers and the vase together for five dollars, but Mary Frances had prevailed on him to let her have just the one feather for a dollar. She thought the vase was vulgar.

She was pleased with the way the chair looked and most particularly pleased with the shimmering green eye of the peacock feather. She placed a copy of Flannery's collected short stories with "Parker's Back" in it on the chair next to the feather. The story was about a man who, in his desperation to win the favor of his aloof and fault-finding wife, wrongly decides to get the face of Jesus tattooed across his back. "Parker's Back" was one of Flannery's last short stories, and as far as Mary Frances was concerned, her best.

"The best," Mary Frances announced aloud to the empty room.

It was the second Friday in Lent and she had been fasting since midnight Thursday. She knew she no longer was required by the Church to fast on the Fridays of Lent, but chose to do so as an act of faith. She loved the way fasting always cast an edge of dizziness over her by dinnertime making her feel cleansed of whatever sins she carried in her thoughts and in her heart. She also liked the rigors and ritual of fasting, and never broke her fast until five past midnight just in case her watch was wrong.

In anticipation of the approach of midnight, she laid out a plate with a single piece of buttered toast and her smallest juice glass filled to the very top with Mogen David wine. The sweet wine was one of the few pleasures she allowed herself during Lent. Her grandmother, who had lived with her and her mother until she died, kept a bottle of Mogen David in her room. Whenever Mary Frances had trouble sleeping, which happened frequently, her grandmother would sneak into her room and give her a small sip of the potent elixir. She did not tell her mother about the hidden bottle of wine or the occasional taste her grandmother gave her, because her mother, God rest her soul, was a bit crazy on the subject of alcohol.

Mary Frances' father had been a drunk. He was not a particularly mean drunk, just a drunk. Mary Frances had never seen him sober, but neither had she seen him sloppy drunk. In general, he was just drunk enough to move a little slower than her mother and to be a little softer spoken, which seemed just about right to Mary Frances. Her mother threw him out for good when Mary Frances was ten.

The morning after her father left, her mother took all his clothes, his books, and his precious jazz records to Catholic Charities. She cleansed the house with Lysol, washing the walls, the shelves, and the floors, as well as every other surface that could survive an ample blessing of Lysol, as though she were ridding the place of some horrible contaminant.

Within twenty-four hours it was as though Mary Frances' father had never been a part of their lives. There was not a trace of him left: not the gentle sway of jazz coming from the turntable in the living room or the sweet cherry smell of his pipe tobacco or even the lingering warm scent of juniper berries from the gin on his breath.

Mary Frances checked her watch. It was three minutes after midnight. She had two minutes to go before she could safely break her fast. She took the box of matches from the stove along with her mother's good silver candlesticks from the buffet and put a fresh white taper in each candlestick. She put the two candles on the seat of the chair. She was careful to place the candles so flames could not accidentally touch the back of the chair or the book. Satisfied, she lit the candles. When she blew out the match, she took it into the kitchen, placed it in the bottom of the sink and ran cold water over it.

She checked her watch again. It was five after midnight.

"Wish me luck, Grandma," she said as she crossed herself before she picked up the glass of sweet wine and the piece of buttered toast.

"The blood of Christ," she muttered to herself before she tipped the glass to her mouth and drank it. "The body of Christ," she announced as she ate the bread.

She went to the cupboard and took out the rosary she kept hidden in her grandmother's silver sugar bowl.

She draped the beads over her hand the way the nuns at Saint Ignatius had taught her to do. She knelt by the chair. Holding the crucifix in both hands, she silently prayed the Creed. She finished with a loud Amen.

Nothing happened.

She touched the edge of the rug with the rosary and said the Our Father. Again, nothing happened. She whispered Flannery O'Connor's name as she held tightly onto the rosary. She took the next rosary bead between her fingers and closed her eyes for the beginning of the three Hail Marys.

"Hail Mary, full of grace," she prayed, her head spinning from the wine, "the Lord is with you. Blessed are you among women, and blessed is the fruit of your womb, JESUS..."

"You lied."

Mary Frances looked up, and there, perched on the top of the chair like a barnyard chicken sitting on a fence, was Mary Flannery O'Connor. Her face looked young, yet there were clear signs of her Lupus: her hands were swollen and her legs looked stiff and awkward. Mary Frances wondered about the Lupus and why it would still be there given that the nuns had always taught her that when you went to heaven your spiritual body was perfect in Christ.

"The Lupus was always there," Flannery spoke out as though she could read Mary Frances' mind, "just waiting for me to discover it, and so it will always be with me."

Flannery let the soft single syllable of "me" drawl out like honey, turning her head to one side as if to preen her feathers. "You've got stuff too. Ev-er-y-bod-y does."

Flannery tossed her head and let her body shake a bit with an inside laugh as though she had been working hard on delivering the word ev-er-y-bod-y as five distinct syllables ever since she had arrived in eternity and was pleased with the results. Just as quickly as she had been pleased and her body relaxed, her head snapped to the side in disapproval and her eyes filled with reproach.

"Yeeew lied," she said, pointing one long crippled finger at Mary Frances.

"Lied?"

"I know you remember the little white lie you told some thirty-five years ago when you were begging for your job at that poor excuse of a girls' finishing school."

Flannery lifted her chin and rolled her eyes in disgust.

"About being Episcopal instead of Catholic?" Mary Frances asked.

"I see ya' keep your rosary in a sugar bowl in the cupboard."

"It's an Episcopal school."

"Do you really think they care?"

"They asked if I was an Episcopalian."

"And you lied."

"I got a job," Mary Frances said, pushing out her chest. "A good job, too. I sent mother and grandmother money until the day they died. I bought myself this house."

"Hmmm," Flannery said, turning her head from side to side in order to take in the full expanse of the pitiful little house. "I guess you can want something so badly you're willing to do anything to get it. But, now that you've had your chance at this job for awhile, seems like you want something else or otherwise you wouldn't be kneeling on this rug working those rosary beads so hard."

"I just wanted someone to talk to."

"Why, I thought you had a whole classroom of ladies to talk to. Fine ladies, like Tiffany Johnson. Why don't you speak to her?" Flannery taunted, leaning forward on the edge of the back of the chair as though she were at the top of some great mountain, looking down at Mary Frances kneeling on her tattered rug.

"She's dumber than a stump, and you know it," Mary Frances protested.

"Ohhhh, I see. You know, my momma always used to say you ought to be careful what you wish for because wishing makes it so. Like this job you wanted so badly. By the way, Jesus doesn't think much about lying."

"I've been a good teacher."

"Tiffany practically broke a nail trying to get to your class on time the other day. Although, I had to admit, that bit about stopping for a moment of prayer for her punctuality was nice."

"Just this minute I was praying you would come talk with me."

"Didn't Jesus say we should pray in secret?"

"There's no one here," Mary Frances started to say.

"But me," Flannery added, laughing and slapping at her leg.

"Once you got here, I quit praying," Mary Frances said defending herself.

"Lord, child, you best think about praying some more. Don't you know calling people back from eternity can get you in a big leaking bucket of trouble?"

"Why did Parker fall in love with that fat-legged woman?"

"You'd like to know, now wouldn't you?"

"And, why did he think she'd love him back if he had that tattoo of Jesus?"

"Always liked that story. Thought it might be a bit too heavy-handed, but I can see now, not heavy-handed enough. Jesus was on Parker's back. His BACK, for pity sake, and he couldn't see him, at least not unless someone held a mirror for him. Now, a mirror can be a lot of things. It can be a looking glass or it can be someone else's eyes. Could be Jesus' eyes, or maybe even a dog's eyes, or the eyes of that fat-legged woman."

"So if you can't see Jesus, you can't see yourself?"

"Like I said, probably not heavy-handed enough. Always thought I was handing my reader a little too much. Thought they ought to work a little harder for their own redemption. Always hated it when things got printed. That's when I knew it was over. Couldn't take back what I said. That's half the reason it took me so long to do anything."

"So did he see himself?"

"Lord, you do want a lot don't you? What all did you ask that tacky rug for?"

"Just you."

"What about Sister Agnes James?"

"I never asked for her."

"You think making her stop yapping in your head just happened by magic?"

"I didn't ask for it."

"What if I told you it wasn't the rug?"

"But you're here."

"Could be this chair or these candles. It could even be that rosary your choking in your hands."

"Could be, but it isn't."

"Seems like it might be time for me to leave."

"Wait. I didn't mean it. It's just that the rug. Sister Agnes James. My father. And now you."

"You could have done it without the rug."

"I didn't know."

"Neither did Parker."

"Did she love him?"

"The way a child loves a crippled cat."

"Was that enough?"

"Depends on what the child wants from the cat."

"I don't think it was enough."

"You might be right. Then again, you might be wrong. That fat-legged woman didn't seem to want much, did she?"

"Would you come talk to my students?"

"Talk to Miss Tiffany?"

"There are others."

"Name one worth talking to. One who's read anything lately other than Cos-mo-pol-i-tan Magazine. Seems to me you got into a little speck of trouble a while back saying something to the faculty about their own lack of in-tel-lec-tu-al in-te-gri-ty and curiosity?"

"That was a mistake."

"A mistake? Were you right or were you wrong in your accusation?"

"I..."

"You were right and you know it. That's what made them so mad. Lawd, we just laughed and laughed at you standing there like you had been thinking about saying that all along and you weren't at all surprised when it just fell out of your mouth. That nasty old thing, what's her name, the one who teaches poetry and always wears the same black dress and same cheap string of pearls everyday like she's either some great sorrowing widow or real poet herself, even though she's never written a poem worth a nickel or anything except for one little pimple of a piece she squeezed out of her dissertation on the 'Metrical Experimentation of Elizabeth Barrett Browning's Poetry.' Now, that was a revelation!"

Flannery slapped her knee again and laughed so hard she nearly fell off the back of the wooden chair.

"You said we, that we laughed..."

"You think I'm the only writer hanging around in heaven? You think I got there because I'm Catholic? I mean, being Catholic didn't hurt and all, but it's not everything."

"Hemingway?"

"He's there. Sylvia is too, and even that scoundrel Shakespeare. You know, you really need to keep a lid on your personal life a little, but all-in-all, heaven is a pretty forgiving place." Again, she laughed. "Forgiving...don't you see?"

"Did the fat-legged woman forgive Parker?"

Flannery leveled her gaze at Mary Frances as though she were the dumbest student in the class and late to boot.

"The point is," Flannery spat out impatiently, "did Parker forgive himself?"

"Yes," Mary Frances said, the rosary slipping one silent bead at a time through her practiced fingers, "Parker had to forgive himself."

"And anyone else who might have stumbled through his tacky life. That is what redemption is all about, not to put too neat a spin on it. Salvation too. Now, I really must be going. Stayed too long it seems. Probably said too much."

"The rug..."

"Most anything can be magic. Depends on your point of view. The Church always went for candles. Cheap and easy to make, a rather dandy symbol if you think about it: the eternal flame and all, light to see the way, warmth and impermanence all wrapped up into one tidy package that can fit into your pocket and go anywhere. Yep, the perfect little bit of magic. Always liked them myself."

"Candles?"

"Never once went to church without lighting one. Always had one to light for one of my peafowl that was looking a bit off the feed. But, sometimes for bigger things like fame, success, redemption, or even a decent conversation. Now, there's something worth asking for."

With that she winked at Mary Frances and disappeared.

Mary Frances looked around the empty room. She wasn't at all surprised by Flannery's quick exit. In fact, the quick exit was just one more proof Flannery had actually been there. Everything

Mary Francis had ever read about Flannery indicated she had an abrupt nature and was not one to linger over unnecessary chitchat. Mary Frances smiled to herself as she worked swiftly through the rest of the rosary. She considered it bad luck not to finish a rosary once she'd started it. Besides, there was no hurry.

All Mary Frances could think about over the weekend was what Flannery had said about candles. She also liked the way a burning candle could set the mood for contemplation. When she was little and her father would take her to Mass without her mother, he would let her light a votive candle all by herself with one of the long church-matches. He'd pick her up in his arms so she could hold her hands just above the flame so the candle would warm them while she prayed. Her mother would have never let her do such a dangerous thing.

Mary Francis had a plan. Her original idea was to have Flannery, as well as some other authors, come talk to the students. But, as she thought more about it over the weekend, she came to believe it would be better to have Flannery and the others talk directly with the faculty rather than the students. Once the faculty was inspired by these great writers and what they had to say, Mary Frances was sure the intellectual life of the St. Mary's School would be renewed.

Her plan was to first summon Flannery and let Flannery take over from there introducing her friends. And, she would do it with candles, not the rug.

She rather liked the elegant touch a tall taper in a candlestick brought to any occasion. However, she only had one set of candlesticks, the silver ones she had used to summon Flannery. One set of candlesticks would not be enough, so Mary Francis revised her original plan and decided to use short stubby votives that could stand up on their on volition and leave her silver candlesticks at home. Mary Frances believed she needed something more akin to the blazing table of candles she had seen when she toured Notre Dame. She was sure such a display of devotion was more like what Flannery was talking about when she talked about forgiveness and redemption and hinted how she liked candles, and also how they could be magic.

Mary Francis had wanted all of the candles to be white, or even cream-colored, like the ones in Notre Dame, so they would have a kind of penitent feel to them. But, neither the party store nor the drugstore had enough white candles to make any difference. So, she had to settle for an odd collection of pillar candles and tea lights including quite a few leftover red and green Christmas candles heavily perfumed with bayberry and pine.

Mary Frances decided she would leave the rug at home. Flannery had said the rug was only magic because Mary Frances wished it to be so. It did bother her, however, that she couldn't remember ever wanting the rug to be magic. It wasn't until after it had actually done something that she thought about it being magic. Flannery had clearly said she didn't need the rug.

Shortly after midnight on Sunday evening, Mary Frances filled two large shopping bags with the candles and a box of kitchen matches. She took the rosary from her grandmother's sugar bowl and put it in her pocket and got into her car and drove to the school.

She knew what she needed to do. Right after she used the candles to call forth the spirits of Flannery and the other authors she would apologize to the faculty for what she had said. She had already forgiven herself for the lie she'd told about being Episcopal, and now she would tell the faculty she forgave them for snubbing her and would invite them all to share in the magic she had discovered.

Once they saw what she had done for them, bringing them the great thinkers and writers they once loved, she believed they would be grateful to her and would embrace her and she would at last be one of them.

She parked her car toward the back of the parking lot and

walked across the campus to the library. She was careful to walk in the shadows so the night watchman wouldn't see her. When she got to the library she used her faculty passkey to unlock the door and let herself in. She didn't turn on the lights because she didn't want the security guard to come along and find her. She wanted this to be a surprise. She wanted it to feel like the best party anyone had ever attended.

She stood by the turnstile for a moment letting her eyes adjust to the dark. There was just enough moonlight coming through the windows so she would be able to gather books and get things set up without turning on any lights.

Once she pushed through the turnstile, she put her heavy bags of candles down on the librarian's desk and went to work pulling books from the stacks, moving tables, and spreading out the chairs in a large half circle. She wanted it to be just perfect, so when the faculty came in for the regular Monday morning meeting, everyone would be able to sit down and see her offering.

Once the chairs were set, she dragged two large wooden tables into the center of the half circle and began standing books up on end on the tables, just as she had done with Flannery's work on the chair, so the titles could be read. And in front of each of the slightly opened, freestanding books, she placed a candle.

She used all the white candles first, but when she ran out of white, she used the red and green ones as well. When she was finished, she placed the remaining colored candles along the edge of the library shelves behind the tables.

It took her nearly three hours to rearrange the furniture, make her book selections and place the candles. Her eyes were tired and her arms felt heavy. The work, however, was good. Satisfying.

They will be so surprised, she thought, so very surprised. It will be like the very best, most beautiful Christmas morning. And when it's over we'll all be new, refreshed, the best of teachers, and the best of friends.

Mary Frances was pleased. The library felt transformed. She looked at the work she'd done and felt both invigorated and pleasingly tired. The soft muffled sounds of the sleeping library, the low hum of the furnace, the shushing of warm air, made her drowsy.

"I should feel tired," she announced proudly to her fine display of books and candles, but even as she said it she knew she couldn't go to sleep. If she did, she might not wake up in time to light the candles before the faculty came for the meeting.

She sat down in the chair nearest the largest table and took the rosary from her pocket. Holding it tightly in her hand, she recited the Glorious Mysteries: Resurrection, Ascension into Heaven, Descent of the Holy Ghost, Assumption, Crowning of Our Blessed Lady, Faith and Hope, Desire of Heaven, The Gifts of the Holy Ghost, Devotion to Mary, Perseverance. Yes, perseverance, she thought. That was what she must have: perseverance. She would stay awake. She would not fall short of her mark. She would do what she had come to do.

But she was tired, so she quickly formulated another plan. She would wait another hour and then she would light the candles and say the rosary as she called forth the great authors and teachers of all time. She would have them waiting there with her for the faculty to discover. They would be so surprised. They would never laugh at her again.

When the clock in the library struck four, she took the box of kitchen matches and began to light the candles. She lit those on the shelves first, then the ones on the table. At each candle she called out a hearty, "Hail Mary, full of grace the Lord is with you and with thy spirit."

When she finished, she sat down on the chair again. The room glowed with flickering light. She held her hands over the nearest candle just as she had done as a child when she was with her father. She had never felt such light and warmth before. It was, just as Flannery had said, magic.

The perfume of the bayberry and pine candles made the room feel full of Christmas and expectation. She let the sweet heavy smell fill her lungs. She breathed deeply and tried to call on the spirits to come. She began to recite the Rosary, letting the beads slip through her fingers as she prayed.

She prayed like she had never prayed before, the rosary warm in her hands, the light of the candles giving her hope. She closed her eyes. First, she prayed out loud to the empty room, and then she prayed silently in her head. As the beads slipped one by one through her fingers, the prayers she whispered were like a beautiful wind blowing through her mind. She couldn't wait for the other faculty members to see the rosary in her hands, to understand she was Catholic, and to see what magic she had done.

She felt happy and redeemed. As the bright flames of the candles filled the room with warmth and hope, her head became drowsy with the richness of bayberry, pine and burning wax. In her heart, she felt like she could pray forever, but her body felt weary. She looked around the room. She was alone. No one would know if she rested her head on the table for a moment. The warmth of the candles covered her like a blanket.

And, then, like so many students have done so many times before in a warm classroom in spring, she let her mind dart for just a flicker of a second into sleep, before she drew it back again to consciousness. Her eyes opened and closed while her fingers still worked the beads. Back and forth her mind swam through the sweet warm smell of the candles moving her from sleep to consciousness until, at last, her mind broke free and found a resting place in a fine deep sleep. She didn't feel her hand hit the first book, or hear the book push against the burning candle, or the candle fall to the floor.

It was so rich a place of blessed sleep she didn't smell the fire as it twisted and rose and carried the spirits she had called forth higher and higher throughout the library, the flames leaping from book to book until the blaze rose and took both Mary Frances and her many ghosts away through the night.

CHAPTER 7

1967
THE HANDYMAN

The eerie warning blast of an oncoming fire truck made Lynwood stop at the corner and wait. A few seconds later, a hook-and-ladder truck blazed through the intersection, made a hasty right turn at the next corner and sped up Saint Mary's Street.

James Powell's familiar fire-chief car followed closely behind.

On any other day, Lynwood would have ignored the fire truck and walked straight up Boylan to go Finch's Restaurant for breakfast. But, things had been slow lately and he didn't have anything to do today other than help James's mother, Mrs. Powell, trim the camellias. Breakfast could wait.

Instead of going straight, he turned left to follow the path of the fire engine. The air around St. Mary's College was filled with smoke. Before he could get to Hillsborough Street, more fire trucks were on their way. Lynwood noticed smoke billowing out of the roof of the library.

James was standing on the lawn shouting orders when he approached.

"Accident?" Lynwood asked.

"Someone was inside when it happened," James answered, keeping his eye on the building as it smoldered and burned.

"Arson?"

"Could be. You can tell by how the smoke has seeped through the windows and pushed up the sides of the building the fire has been burning for two, maybe three hours already. Roof is nearly gone. Got the alarm at six. Janitor noticed when he came to work and called it in. You would have thought one of the girls in the dorms might have smelled the smoke last night and called someone. Could have done something about it if we could have gotten here earlier. All those books. Kindling, really."

Lynwood looked around the parking lot. It was empty except for one car.

"Is that Mary Frances' car?"

James looked where Lynwood was pointing.

"Sure looks like it."

"She teaches here."

"English, right?"

"I wash her porch every Sunday afternoon even if it's raining. Keeps her porch so clean you could eat off it. Washed it just yesterday. Said she'd pay me today."

"Daryl," James called out to one of his men, "you say you think there's a body in there?"

"Yeah. Dead for sure. It's like a furnace in there. We called out when we broke down the door. Saw something that looked like a body slumped across a table. Pretty badly burned up. Got no answer. No chance they're still alive. Joe tried to go in, but it was just too damn hot."

The hook and ladder took the hose high up into the air and sent a shower of water onto the roof of the building.

"Get those windows knocked out," James called to the men on the ground.

The men grabbed axes and began working their way down the sides of the building breaking windows. Flames leaped out of the windows with a whoosh of heat and smoke.

"When will you know?" Lynwood asked.

"Know what?"

"If it's Mary Frances."

It was well past nine o'clock when Lynwood finally got to Finch's. He took his regular seat at the end of the counter.

"Hey," Maxine called from across the room, "I was worried you might be out on a bender." She grabbed a clean coffee mug, filled it halfway with black coffee and set it in front of Lynwood.

"There was a fire," Lynwood said, pouring enough cream and sugar into the cup to bring the coffee to the brim.

"Thought I smelled something burning."

"The library at St. Mary's."

"All them books…"

"Someone was in the library."

"Good Lord! Who?"

"Mary Frances' car was there, in the parking lot."

"You think it was her?"

"James said he thought the place had been burning for a couple of hours before it was called in. Doesn't seem like anyone could have survived."

"Oh, my God, Mary Frances…"

Lynwood took the long way back, walking down St. Mary's Street again instead of Boylan. The fire trucks were still there. A crowd of students had gathered. Lynwood stood at the edge looking for James.

James saw him, and waved him over.

"We think it might be Mary Frances," he said, pointing towards the ambulance.

Lynwood closed his eyes, shoved his hands deep into his pockets.

"She's badly burned. Any next of kin?"

"A cousin named Jo. Visits Mary Frances sometimes. Fancy lady. Lives in Manhattan."

"I hate to ask this Lynwood, but I need you to look, to make sure it's Mary Frances."

"She told me to come by today, said she was going to pay me as soon as she got home. Yesterday, I cleaned her porch…"

"I know," said James as he put his arm around Lynwood's shoulders and led him towards the ambulance.

It was almost noon when Lynwood got back home to Mrs. Powell's. She was out in the yard working on the camellias. She'd been waiting for him.

"I heard," was all she said.

"It was Mary Frances," Lynwood said.

"People are going to be coming round. You got the key?"

Lynwood had a key for Mary Frances' house. He also had keys to Mrs. Powell's, Addie Walker's, and old Mr. Jenkins' place at the foot of Kinsey Street by the elementary school. The new people, the ones who moved into the neighborhood when the old ones died or left, didn't trust him with their house keys.

"She won't like people coming in her house," Lynwood cautioned.

"Someone needs to go over there and tidy up, make sure things are right," she said.

Lynwood bent down and pulled up a clump of onion grass at the edge of the lawn.

"You want me to come with you?" she asked.

"No," he said, "I'll go. Mary Frances would want me to clean up before anyone saw her house."

Lynwood filled his wheelbarrow with tools and went over to Mary Frances'. He raked the lawn, trimmed the camellia bushes around her front porch and swept the walkway. He also took the liberty of cutting back a particularly scraggy-looking lilac bush along the side of the house. He'd felt for a long time that the bush wasn't doing well and would benefit from some serious pruning, but Mary Frances had refused to hear of it.

When he was satisfied Mary Frances would be happy with the way her yard looked, except for the now-shortened and, he thought, healthier-looking lilac bush, he put the tools into his wheelbarrow. Out of habit, before he put the key in the lock, he knocked on the door.

"Miss Mary Frances..." Lynwood called out to the empty

house.

He unlocked the door, pushed it wide open and stepped out of the way. He waited a minute, not believing in ghosts, but hoping if Mary Frances' spirit was still in the house, it would have the good sense to rush out into the sunlight and escape.

"Hello," he called out again. No one answered.

The room was still and felt odd the way an empty house always feels when its owner was gone. When his eyes became accustomed to the darkened room, he saw one of Mary Frances' good dining-room chairs in the middle of the living room sitting on a small oriental rug. Lynwood recognized it as the rug she had brought back from her recent trip to Boston. There was a pair of silver candlesticks with half-burned candles, a peacock feather and a book on the seat of the chair. The set-up looked a whole lot like witchcraft.

Lynwood closed the front door so no one would see what he had found. With the door closed, the room suddenly felt warm and heady with a faint smell of burned candle wax. James had told him there were traces of candle wax all around Mary Frances when they took her body out of the library.

"What on earth, Mary Frances?" Lynwood asked the empty room.

There were books and scraps of paper scattered around the edges of the rug as if someone had thrown them about like rose petals. Lynwood picked up the books, all the while stepping gingerly around the rug as though it might burst into flames. He put the books that were on the floor back into the bookshelf.

When he bent down to pick up the scraps of paper, he saw Mary Frances had written names on them: Shakespeare, Hemingway, Steinbeck, Jane Austin, Gertrude Stein, Sir Arthur Conan Doyle, Sylvia Plath, Flannery O'Connor. He took all the little bits of paper into the kitchen and threw them in the trash.

On the counter near the trashcan, he found a dirty glass next to a nearly empty bottle of Mogen David wine. He picked up the dirty glass and saw there was a dark red splotch of wine, not yet fully dried, on the bottom of the glass.

It had been more than a year since he'd had anything to drink. One year since his last, as Maxine had put it this morning, "bender."

He rubbed his hand down the front of his shirt, touched the small puddle of wine in the bottom of the glass and put his finger on the tip of his tongue; sweet, warm the way a shot of whiskey drunk too fast can burn your lungs. He poured the rest of the bottle into the dirty glass.

With glass in hand, he opened the cupboards looking to see if Mary Frances kept any other secrets around. There on the top shelf was a second, unopened bottle of Mogen David.

"Wouldn't want James to know about them candlesticks on that chair, or Mrs. Powell and the others to know Miss Mary Frances had a taste for the grape," Lynwood said. "No, no, no, Miss Mary Frances would not like that, no sir, no indeed."

He polished off what he had already poured into his glass and took the other bottle from the shelf. He twisted the cap off the new bottle and pushed the first empty bottle deep into the trash.

He promised himself he'd have only another glass or two, hardly enough to make a difference. Once things were in good order, he'd take the rest of the bottle back to his apartment and finish it there.

He couldn't risk getting drunk. At least not yet. He had liked Mary Frances. She sometimes loaned him books and always talked to him in a way that made him feel he was just like her and had been to school. He wanted to do right by her, make sure things were in order for her colleagues and neighbors, or others who thought they knew her, to come and poke around her private life.

That's what people did when they came into the homes of the dead. They poked around, opened drawers, peeked into medicine cabinets, drank in the shock of their discoveries, and when no one was looking, rummaged through the closets.

Lynwood tried not to judge people, but the thought of people looking through Mary Frances' neat little house disgusted him. He figured they did what they did because they were scared of being alone when they died and were worried about what it might be like to be dead themselves and have everything they once loved left behind for others to touch.

Lynwood knew people sometimes talked about Mary Frances behind her back and made fun of her. Mary Frances had been nothing but kind to him and he didn't want anyone gossiping about her, so he took his time emptying the various trashcans in the house, scrubbing the bathroom and cleaning out the refrigerator and the medicine cabinet. He tidied up the bedroom, made her bed and hung up the bathrobe Mary Frances had left on the chair.

He had never imagined Mary Frances was the kind of woman to burn down a library on purpose, or to get out of a bed and not make it. He took extra care to smooth the covers and tuck the pillows neatly under the pink satin coverlet so no one would know.

When he finished in her bedroom, he went back to the kitchen and poured another glass of wine, this time, full, up to the top, the way he liked to do when he fixed his coffee. He took a long deep sip in order to keep the wine from spilling when he walked across the kitchen. He carried his glass into the living room and sat down so he could take a good look at things. He needed to think about what to do about the chair, the candlesticks and the rug.

For sure, he couldn't tell James or anyone else about them. There was something funny about all of it: the fire at the library, Mary Frances being there alone in the middle of the night, the strange little altar she'd made of the chair and the rug she'd just bought sitting in the middle of the living room. And then there was the issue of the candles on the chair and the candle wax in the library. Like her unmade bed, all of it needed to be cleaned up and pushed aside like some terrible secret he'd have to keep.

Mary Frances was the fourth customer he'd lost in the last year. Mrs. Ritter and Mr. Rhodes had died over the summer, and last month, Mrs. Mayes moved to a nursing home. Whenever one of his customers died or moved to a nursing home, the new people never hired him: treated him like a thief.

"I charged Mrs. Ritter $20 to clean the gutters," he told the new owner when he came by last week to return the key Mrs. Ritter had given him, "and $10 to wash her porch each week."

The woman took the key from Lynwood's outstretched hand, careful not to touch him.

"Just $10 to clean the porch," he told her.

The woman didn't speak, but stood in her doorway, hand on the doorknob looking at his faded clothes and rough hands like she might call the police if he took one step closer.

"Just $10 a week," Lynwood had said again, "I can do yours on Sunday afternoon, same time I do Miss Mary Frances'. Once a week keeps it clean, good-looking. I do Mrs. Powell's too. You can trust me. I do lots of porches in Boylan Heights. Ask anyone."

Just $10, and she said no.

With Mrs. Mayes in the nursing home, Mr. Rhodes and Mrs. Ritter dead, and now Mary Frances gone as well, there were only three houses left in the neighborhood for him to take care of, and one of those was Mrs. Powell's. Mrs. Powell didn't really count, however, because she didn't pay him. Instead, he traded her work around her place for rent in her basement apartment.

Three porches to wash, gutters to keep clear, sidewalks to sweep and basements to clean. Hardly enough work to give him money to eat breakfast every morning at Finch's.

Mary Frances owed him money. $10 for the porch, another $15 or so today for trimming her bushes and sweeping the front walk, not to mention cleaning out her refrigerator and picking up around the house.

Lynwood walked into the kitchen, poured a little more wine into his glass and rummaged around in the trash until he found a slip of paper. He took a pencil from the drawer near the telephone.

"Ten for cleaning the porch yesterday," he announced to the empty room. "Another $15 for trimming the bushes and sweeping the front porch makes $25."

Lynwood wrote down the figures and circled the total.

Mary Frances owed him money and she was gone. He polished off what wine was left in his glass and began searching through the kitchen drawers. He found three pennies and a nickel in the drawer by the phone, but that was all.

He went to the dining room and looked in the china hutch. Nothing. He went to the bedroom and looked in her dresser drawers, pulling out shirts, socks and underwear. Nothing. He looked in her closet and found the handbag he'd seen her carry when she went somewhere fancy.

He opened the bag and shook out the contents onto her bed. Two red striped mints and a torn ticket stub for "Annie" at the Gershwin Theatre in New York fell out of the bag, along with two neatly folded one-dollar bills. The bills were folded such that Lynwood could easily imagine Mary Frances had done it so she could grab the money out of her purse without having to look when she needed to tip a porter or a cab driver.

Mary Frances was always so careful to pay what she owed.

He put the folded bills in his pocket and put the mints and the ticket stub back into the purse and snapped it shut. He put the purse back in the closet, picked up the clothes off the floor that he'd pulled from her dresser, and pushed them back into the drawers.

Mary Frances still owed him $22.92. He went to the kitchen and poured the rest of the Mogen David into his glass and went back into the living room. His head was feeling warm and flushed and just a touch dizzy from the sweet-tasting wine. He sat down in the big chair and turned on the reading lamp.

The afternoon sun was just beginning to fade and the room was growing dark. He looked at the little altar Mary Frances had put together with the chair, the candlesticks and the rug. What had Mary Frances needed to pray for? Why had they found candle wax in the library?

Lynwood really needed the money Mary Frances owed him. He thought maybe he could take the candlesticks in payment. For sure, Mary Frances had no more use for them. Plus, if he took the candlesticks, then no one would ever think Mary Frances was some kind of pyromaniac who prayed for strength to burn the library down. Taking the candlesticks would be doing her a favor.

Maybe he'd take the candlesticks along with a book or two. He didn't know how much a book might cost, but figured the candlesticks were good for at least $15 or $20.

He decided he'd take only two books. That seemed right to Lynwood: the candlesticks and two books, and he and Mary Frances would be square.

All this thinking and figuring was making him feel thirsty. He took another good long sip of wine and got up from the chair. He ran his hand down the spines of the books tucked neatly into the bookcase: Shakespeare, Dostoyevsky, Mark Twain, Sylvia Plath, Willa Cather, James Joyce. He tapped each one as he walked down the bookshelf, trying to judge by the firmness of their spines which two books would be the best to take.

They all felt the same. He kept tapping. Towards the end of the row, he came to a dark blue book that was different than the rest. The writing on the spine said *Reader's Digest Condensed Book*. He'd seen such books in some of the other houses he cared for, but couldn't remember ever seeing Mary Frances reading this particular type of book. He tapped his index finger against the gilt letter binding trying to figure if it was one of the books he should take. He tapped it once and then a second time. It sounded different than the others.

He tapped the *Reader's Digest* again: it had an odd hollow sound to it. He pulled it off the shelf. The edges of the book where there should have been pages were not pages at all, but more like the sides of a box. The three sides were smooth and covered in gold foil. The front cover felt like it was a lid to the box. He tried to open it. He could see it could come open, but was stuck a bit like there was some latch or something inside keeping it shut. He tried again, this time harder. The book opened. A flutter of bills fell to the floor. It wasn't a book at all, but a box dressed up to look like a book where Mary Frances had hidden money.

Lynwood knelt down and spread the money out on the floor. There were $20s, $10s and a few $5s, clipped together with paperclips in neat packets of $100. There were ten packets in all: $1,000. He had never in his life had $1,000 at one time to hold. He picked up the money. He was surprised by how light it felt. He had never imagined so much money could be bundled small enough to fit into the hollow of a book.

He put the money back inside the book and closed the cover tightly so it would catch and latch.

"Is this the book you want me to take?" he called out to the empty room, half expecting Mary Frances to answer.

The clock in the corner chimed the hour: 6 o'clock. It was starting to get dark. The room was still.

"You told me to come by today, said you'd pay me, remember?"

Lynwood ran his rough hands across the smooth blue cover of the book.

"I'll pray about it," he offered.

It had been a long time since Lynwood had gotten on his knees and prayed. It wasn't that he didn't believe, just that he didn't believe anyone would hear the prayers of someone like him.

He knelt on the rug and put the blue *Reader's Digest* on top of the book by Flannery O'Connor. He fumbled in his pocket for a pack of matches and lit the candle stubs.

The candlelight warmed the room. Lynwood's head felt dizzy with the wine and the smell of the burning wax. He sat back on his heels and let his hands drift to the rug. He rubbed the silken nap with his fingers. It was thin to the touch as though a hundred people had already rubbed their hands against its soft fibers, asking for something.

"Can you hear me, Mary Frances?"

He had a sudden urge to press his face to the rug. He blew out the candles and pushed the chair, hard, out of the way. One of the chair legs caught a thread and ripped a quick hole at the corner of the rug.

He put his cheek against the small mihrab on the rug and let his hands rest on the two squares of woven flowers. The beating in his heart slowed and calmed.

"I won't take your candlesticks. I'm not a thief. I took Mrs. Ritter's blue glass paperweight after she died, but only because she always told me it was to be mine. She said she wanted me to have it if she ever died, as if she wasn't sure dying was something that would happen to her. She told me once she was afraid of dying, afraid her daughter would just throw all her beautiful things away. She told me to take the paperweight, she did I swear it. And, when I took Mr. Rhode's clothes to Goodwill to get rid of them, I kept that one sweater. It was nothing special, just an old grey sweater. You told me you'd pay me today. Do you want me to have the money you left? Did you help me find the book? I'm sorry the library burned down. I'm sorry I tore your rug. I'm so very sorry you're gone."

He closed his eyes and waited. The room felt warm, his arms suddenly heavy by his sides. He waited for Mary Frances to speak to him. When no answer came, he got up from the rug and took the two candlesticks into the kitchen to clean the wax from them so no one would know what either he or Mary Frances had done.

Once cleaned and polished, he put the candlesticks back into the china hutch where he had remembered seeing them before. He put the peacock feather in the trash and took the chair back into the dining room. He picked up the rug and gave it a gentle shake as if he were trying to coax an answer out of it.

He remembered seeing a sewing kit in the bathroom when he cleaned the medicine cabinet. He found the kit, threaded a needle with a light-tan-colored thread and carefully, tiny stitch by tiny stitch, repaired the rug. His mother had been a seamstress and had taught him to sew when he was ten. He felt a certain satisfaction knowing he was good at making tiny stitches and could repair what he had damaged. It was a beautiful rug.

"Good as new," he said as he knotted the last stitch and bit through the thread, breathing in the smell of dust and the faint remnant of desert sand.

He put the rug at the foot of Mary Frances' bed and the sewing kit back in its place in her medicine cabinet. He walked through the house one more time taking a careful look to be sure everything was neat and tidy and in its rightful place. He wanted things to be perfect for the visitation after the funeral.

He tied up the trash bag and put it in his wheelbarrow to take back to Mrs. Powell's. He washed his now empty glass and put it in the cupboard. He wiped down the countertops and cleaned the sink.

The two books, the one by Flannery O'Connor and the hollow *Reader's Digest* filled with money, were sitting on the coffee table where he'd left them.

"No one is ever going to know about the candlesticks and the altar, Mary Frances. No one is ever going to know about you or me kneeling on the rug and praying for things. It'll be our secret. No one is ever going to know," he said.

He reached into his pocket and felt for Mary Frances' key. It felt warm in his hand. "Tell me what you want me to do. Give me a sign."

Nothing. He picked up the book by Flannery O'Connor and decided he'd take it home with him.

He looked at the *Reader's Digest*.

"I'm not a thief, I won't take the other book unless you want me to have it. Do you? Do you want me to have it?"

He picked up the book, pulled at its tight cover, and took one more look at the money inside.

"You said you were going to pay me today. You owe me $25."

His hands started to shake and sweat broke out on his forehead. He put the hollow book back down on the coffee table and ran his fingers through the money. He pulled a $20 from one stack of bills and a $5 from another. He reached into his pocket and pulled out the two folded bills he found in her purse and the coins from the kitchen drawer, and dropped them into the box.

"I'm not a thief," he said as he closed the book and slipped it back into its place on the bookshelf. "I'm not a thief."

CHAPTER 8

1967
THE SHRINK

Jo unrolled the small prayer rug.

"What do you think?" she asked her husband.

"About?"

"The rug."

He took a quick look and turned his attention back to the book he was reading.

"Well?"

"What is it about shrinks and oriental rugs?" he asked.

She ignored her husband and smoothed the worn edges of the old rug with her hands.

"They're pretty to look at; something to talk about when things get complicated."

"Where are you going to put it?"

"In my office."

"I thought you were quitting."

"It's complicated."

Her cousin, Mary Frances, had told her about the rug the last time they talked. She said it was a magic rug. They had a good laugh together about her finding it in a junk store in Boston.

"Only you," she had told Mary Frances, "could find such a rug."

"And only $10!" Mary Frances had boasted.

"I charge my clients a lot more than that for magic," she had told her.

Mary Frances then said something about hearing voices.

"Do you think I'm crazy?" she had asked Jo.

"Lots of people hear voices, talk to themselves, even have

conversations in their heads with the dead. It's normal. That said, I wouldn't tell anyone."

The rug was unlike anything else Mary Frances had ever owned. It was not at all like the heavy overstuffed furniture and dreary old paintings of English cottages and seascapes Mary Frances had inherited from her mother, or her bookcase crammed with books. The rug felt light and airy and pulsing with energy, like it could, if it could only get outside, fly.

The rug felt as though it was real in a way Jo couldn't quite explain. Maybe Mary Frances was right: it was magic. The last thing the two of them had talked about was the rug and how happy it seemed to make Mary Frances. Mary Frances had not always been happy in her life. Jo regretted she hadn't called her cousin more often.

Jo had a modern Turkish rug done in soft pastel hues in her office. The decorator had bought it. Jo didn't particularly like it. In fact, she wouldn't have chosen it for herself, but that was the point. Like everything else in her carefully designed office, it said nothing about who she was and faded ghost-like into the background.

When Jo took Mary Frances' tattered red and smoky-black tribal rug to her office, she put it on top of the pale pastel one: near the couch and her chairs. In contrast to the decorator rug, the old one felt alive and bold. She liked how it looked in the room. It seemed inviting. It wouldn't have surprised her at all if one of her clients might not want to kneel down on it and pray.

The phone in her office rang.

"Jo-Jo!"

"No," she said.

"Come on, it's just one..."

"One more truly crazy crafty client you can't handle, right?"

"But, you're the shrink of last resort. You're the best, damn it."

Jo could hear Dr. Allen Abrams lean forward in his big leather chair. Heard the soft thud of his fist hit his desk.

"Nice try, I'm not buying." Jo checked her watch. She didn't have another client coming in for another 40 minutes.

"She needs a woman's touch. Hates men. Hates me right now. Too much transference too fast, I'm not doing her any good. Husband left her for a younger woman."

"Same ol', same ol'. Look, got to go, got a client arriving," Jo lied.

"Your secretary said you were free for at least another half hour. Let's talk."

"Nope, nyet, no. I've had my fill of crazies lately, thinking about getting out of the business."

"Yeah, yeah, yeah..."

"For real," Jo said.

"What are you going to do? Take up yoga? Learn to tap dance?"

"Thought I'd go on vacation with Tom. You remember, Tom, my husband, your best friend: the one who has been bugging me for the last ten years to quit my practice and travel the world with him? He wants to retire."

"Let him, but first, do me this one last favor and take this client."

"Ask someone else."

"She needs you."

"No she doesn't."

"Just see her once, that's all I'm asking. Once, and if you think you can't handle it, if you think you're not that good anymore and you can't solve her problems and save the world from her paranoid, probably psychotic, maybe even narcissistic self, you can send her back."

"She sounds charming," Jo said, wishing she hadn't answered the phone.

"Hardly, but she pays in cash."

Jo really had thought about quitting. Not just because of Tom, but because it had gotten harder with all the paperwork, the pressure to take more and more clients in order to pay the bills, and all the hassles with insurance companies. But, most of all, she wanted to quit because she was tired of keeping other people's secrets.

"And if I say yes?" Jo asked.

"I'm sending you her file right now," Allen replied.

"I didn't say yes," Jo said.

"But you're thinking about it and with you a think is as good as a yes."

"This is the last time..."

"Promise."

"I mean it," Jo said.

"I owe you one."

The client Abrams had thrown at her was in her late fifties, but looked older. If Jo had had to guess, she would have said 67 or 68. The woman was heavy set and puffy in the kind of way some women, who have once been thin and good-looking when they were younger, get when their lives take a wrong turn.

Allen had written in his files that the woman had once done some acting, local stuff, and was proud of it. It had surprised Jo: the woman didn't carry herself like she was either an actress or proud of herself.

When she came in for her appointment, the woman walked into the room like she was pushing a heavy plow across a field. Her clothes seemed wrong: flouncy layers of see-through lace and ruffles stretched tight across her thick midriff. Jo could see the shadow of her heavy legs through the thin gauze of her skirt.

The woman's hair was thin, tangled, shoulder-length and lifeless. She dyed her hair a wrong shade of auburn. Her grey roots showed.

In contrast to her unkempt hair, the woman's nails were nicely manicured and her fingers were heavily jeweled with rings, lots of rings. Some were costume jewelry, others real: all of them big and gaudy. It made Jo think about one of her clients who had gotten so mad when she found out her husband was cheating on her, that she went to the bank, withdrew all the money in their joint accounts and spent every penny of it on a dozen or so big honking diamond rings.

"You need to get something straight," the woman said before she had made her way across Jo's office to drop herself down in the chair beside Jo's desk, "whatever that spineless prick told you about me was a lie. I'm the truth teller here. I know my rights."

"No one told me anything," Jo said calmly.

"You're not my first shrink," the woman said, narrowing her eyes at Jo, "so, just cut the crap. I'll save you some trouble: there's nothing wrong with me. I'm just pissed off that I got dumped."

"Why don't you tell me a little about yourself?"

The woman shook her head, pushed herself back in her chair and took a good look around the room.

"You ought to fire whoever does your decorating," she said, pointing to the dark red prayer rug resting on Jo's larger pastel rug.

"Why do you say that?" Jo asked.

"Any third-grade fool knows you don't put pink and red together. And please don't tell me you paid good money for that moth-eaten rag of a thing. You a Muslim or something?"

"Dr. Abrams thought..." Jo started to say.

"Abrams is a piece of work. Thinks he's God's own special gift to women – just like my ex."

"Tell me about your divorce." Jo prompted.

"Wouldn't you like to know..."

"I would."

"Abrams tried to come on to me," the woman said, picking at the edge of one of the ruffles in her skirt, "I wouldn't have it. That's how you got me. Dumped me, just like my ex-husband did. Prick."

"How long had you and your husband been married?"

"If you asked him, he'd probably say too long. Me? I say not long enough, if you know what I mean."

"What do you mean?"

"'til death do us part would have seemed about right to me: his death, not mine!"

"What were you thinking when you just said, 'his death'?"

"Thinking I should have killed him. Couldn't keep his pants zipped and got this big-tit blonde teenager he was bonking pregnant in a BIG way."

The woman joined her hands out in front of her like she was trying to hold a big barrel of something on her lap. She started to cackle.

"Twins. Saw the four of them once. He was pushing the twins in a stroller all the while looking at HER with a shit-eating grin on his face like she was some kind of fertility goddess and his sperm was magic!"

"Do you have children?"

"Children don't make you a woman," she snapped.

"How do you feel about being a woman?" Jo asked.

The woman twisted in her chair as if she was looking for something.

"Time's up," the woman said. "Here's my secret. You can keep it if you want. Bought some ant poison with arsenic in it. Thought about killing him." The woman rocked forward in her seat as though she had to get some momentum going in order to propel herself out of the chair, "Planned to mix it in his seedless raspberry jam and spread it on his toast. Seedless! Like he was something special and shouldn't have to pick seeds out of his teeth like everyone else. What a prince! Every morning: two over easy, and two pieces of toast spread edge to edge with SEEDLESS raspberry jam, like I was some kind of short-order cook and he was just passing through."

Jo waited.

"You gonna tell the cops?"

"Should I?"

"I just told you my one big secret and you're asking me if you should call the cops? What kind of shrink are you?"

"I can keep your secret if that's what you want."

The woman opened her purse, pulled out a wad of cash and slapped it on Jo's desk.

"Same time next week?"

Jo checked her calendar, wishing with all her heart that she would be so overbooked she'd have to say no.

"Same time," she said.

"You didn't tell me everything," Jo said.

"She told you about the seedless raspberry jam," Abrams said, leaning back in his chair.

"And that you came on to her."

Jo didn't believe for a second Abrams had made any kind of advance.

"I told you she needed you."

"Would she?"

"Poison him?"

"I'm asking."

"I don't doubt for a moment she wanted to kill him, but she didn't, did she?"

"What if he comes back?"

Abrams considered the question.

"You've met her. You think he's coming back?"

"No."

"Even if he did come back, I don't think she'd do it," Abrams said, sitting up in his chair.

"You're saying not to call the cops?"

"She's got issues, for sure, being dumped for another woman and all, but if we called the cops every time someone told us they wanted to kill their husbands for dumping them, they'd have to quadruple the number of cops on the force and we'd lose our licenses to practice psychological voodoo."

"So, I keep her secret?"

"Right now, she just hates herself. The rest of us are just fodder."

Jo hung up the phone and wrote four words on a piece of paper: anger, fear, shame and secrets. She began matching and crossing off letters: a little obsessive habit she had carried over from high school.

"And the greatest of these," she announced to her empty office, "is secrets."

Lynwood had a secret.

The day after the funeral, he'd come over to Mary Frances' house to help Jo sort through closets and pack up most of it to go to the Goodwill. They'd pretty much pulled all the food from the cupboards and boxed up the pots and pans in the kitchen and were working their way into the dining room when Lynwood spoke.

"James, the fire chief, Mrs. Powell's son, he was the one who asked me to look at her, make sure it was Mary Frances," he said.

"Sorry you had to do that," Jo said, pulling the china from the cupboard: stacking it on the dining table.

"She was burned up bad," Lynwood said, rubbing his hands on his shirt as though just talking about it had made his hands dirty.

"It was a terrible thing, just terrible," Jo said trying hard not to remember saying goodbye to Mary Frances in the funeral home before they put her in her casket and closed the lid.

"Did James tell you?" Lynwood's voice suddenly trailed off as though he was about to say something he shouldn't.

"Tell me what?" Jo stopped what she was doing and sat down

on one of the dining room chairs so she could look at Lynwood.

"About the wax."

"Wax?"

"Lots of wax, all around her. That's what they found. That and all them burned up books."

Jo sat quietly thinking about what he had just said, about the wax.

"James never asked and I never told him. Kept it to myself."

"What didn't you tell him?" Jo asked.

"It's a secret," Lynwood said.

"You can tell me. She was my only cousin."

"You won't tell James or Mrs. Powell, will you? I don't think Mary Frances would have wanted anyone else to know."

"I can keep a secret," Jo told him.

"I had a key. Mrs. Powell told me to put things right in the house, trim the bushes, sweep the walk and stuff."

"You did a nice job, thank you."

"No thanks to it," he said, looking around the room for some way he could tell her what he couldn't hold anymore.

"And?" Jo waited.

"I found something."

"What?"

"It was in the house, there, in the middle of the living room. This chair on that rug, the old red one you said you wanted. They were in the living room."

"She was probably trying to figure out where to put it, is all," Jo assured him.

Lynwood turned his head away.

"The chair was on the rug in the middle of the room, like I told you. And there was a book on the seat of the chair and them candlesticks there," he said, pointing to the silver candlesticks in the china cupboard.

"Could you show me the book?" Jo asked, trying hard not to think about the candlesticks.

"It was by Flannery O'Connor," he said, "I took it home."

"I'm sure Mary Frances would have wanted you to have that book. I'm glad you took it. It's nothing to worry about."

"There were candles in the candlesticks. They'd been burned recently. I could smell it when I walked into the room. There was a feather on the chair too."

"A feather?"

"Peacock. Looked like witchcraft to me, with that feather and all and them burned up candles."

"You didn't tell the fire chief or Mrs. Powell?"

"Didn't tell no one but you."

"Flannery O'Connor was one of her favorites," Jo said, trying fast to sort through the book, the candles, the feather and what it all meant.

"She trusted me with her books, talked to me like I was as good as her."

"She loved books," Jo said in her best shrink manner.

"Can't imagine she meant to burn down the library on purpose," Lynwood offered.

"I can't either."

"I didn't want people talking, that's all, just didn't want them talking," Lynwood said.

"People will talk," Jo agreed.

"What do you think?"

"I don't think Mary Frances would want people to know," Jo offered.

"It's a secret, right?"

"Yes," Jo said, "let's make it our secret."

Jo didn't say anything else, just waited. She knew how much a secret could burn in you and how once you let it out there was like this hole where other things could come out as well.

"There's something else," Lynwood said, walking into the living room. Jo followed him.

"You see this book here," he said, pointing to the spine of the

Reader's Digest.

"Yes." Jo could not quite imagine her cousin ever buying something like a *Reader's Digest,* couldn't imagine Mary Frances choosing to read a condensed book rather than the real thing. Couldn't imagine why she had the book on her shelf.

"It's not a book." Lynwood pulled out the book and showed Jo the smooth gold foil edges. "Mary Frances owed me money, $25, for washing her front porch, did it on the Sunday before the fire. She said I should come by Monday to get paid. Since she wasn't there to pay me, I was thinking I'd take a couple of books to make up for the money she owed me. That's when I found this."

Lynwood gently pulled the cover open and showed Jo the money.

Jo couldn't believe what he was showing her.

"How much?" Jo asked, fascinated that Mary Frances had kept things secret from her and had hidden money inside a book.

"There was a thousand dollars, but I took the $25 she owed me. Put the $2.08 I found in the kitchen when I was cleaning up into the box, so there's $977.08 now."

"You took $25?"

"You can count it if you want, I'm not a thief."

"Of course you're not." Jo was thinking about the fire in the library.

"Only three people left," Lynwood said.

"Three people who know?"

"Only three people left who let me clean their porches. New ones don't trust me."

Jo looked at the box and the money.

"Tell you what," she said, holding out her hand, "how about if I keep the box and you keep the money."

The woman came back the next week just as promised. She was on time. Her hair was still a shocking color of auburn, but it was brushed back away from her face and looked clean.

"Feeling better?" Jo asked.

"Better than what?" the woman challenged.

"Better than last week."

"I'm still divorced if that's what you're asking," she said, plopping down on the couch. The woman kicked off her shoes and put her feet up, letting her body stretch out on the couch. Jo got up from her chair and pulled it into position so she could look at the woman when they talked.

"So," Jo prompted.

"He took up with this three-year-old," the woman said.

"A child?"

"Don't get all literal on me. She was grown, but had the mind of a child to spread her legs for that creep."

"Did you like him?"

"Who?"

"It sounds like you didn't think much of your husband," Jo said.

"Do you?"

"I don't know anything about your husband."

"I was asking about yours," the woman said, crossing her legs and leaning back on the sofa as though she was waiting for an answer.

"We're not here to talk about my husband," Jo said.

"You probably eat your raspberry jam without seeds just like him, like you're better than everyone else. You even look at me like he looked at me. Like I was just a big fat nothing. Well, I know my rights, and I don't have to put up with you and your sneaky questions. In case you've forgotten, I'm the one paying you to answer MY questions!"

Jo suddenly felt tired. And weary. She didn't want to talk anymore, and she didn't want to listen anymore. She just wanted the woman to go away.

"You hear me?" the woman shouted.

Jo didn't say anything and she didn't move. The woman leaned forward and balled up her fists as though she might lurch forward and hit Jo.

"Maybe you'd like to see someone else," Jo said quietly, closing her notebook.

"You can't throw me out," the woman said, her voice tight and shrill, "I know my rights."

"Leave," Jo said as calmly as she could, "please leave."

The woman reached into her pocketbook and pulled out a fistful of bills and threw them on the floor. She tucked her purse under her arm and jammed her feet into her shoes. "I'm coming back," she screamed, "you can't stop me!"

Jo waited until she heard the woman's heavy footsteps go down the hall to the elevator. When she was sure the woman was gone, Jo got up from her chair, locked her office door and turned off the lights. She went to her desk, opened the bottom left-hand drawer and pulled out the *Reader's Digest* box. She took the box, her notebook and a ballpoint pen and sat down on the floor on Mary Frances' rug.

"Bought ant poison with arsenic," she wrote, "planned to kill her husband."

Jo tore off the piece of paper she'd written on, folded it into a tight neat square and put it in the box with the others. The box was already almost full.

"I've got your secret, Mary Frances," Jo said to the dark room. "I'm going to keep it with the others in your hiding box. I'll never tell anyone. I promise, I'll never tell."

CHAPTER 9

1980
THE LOVERS

"Let's have a go at this," Colin said, tossing his old straw hat into the corner and taking a seat on the edge of the big wooden desk.

"A go at it?" Karen stood back and glared at him.

She tried for one of those "if looks could kill" kind of stares, but knew she'd missed. She had once thought Colin's incessant "let's have a go at it" Australian way was charming. But this wasn't about changing flat tires or running to make a bus connection or cooking lobster, this was about the rugs. This was about the end of their long wild marriage. This was about her life.

"Look, now," Colin managed with a laugh, "you agreed we'd do this without the solicitors. Never knew why in bloody hell you insisted on having them mucking around our business in the first place. But I went along, and now it's your turn to go along with 'the plan,' as you say."

"The plan," Karen jabbed, "was for us to get married, have a successful business, and grow old together. So, how do you think we should proceed?" she said, smiling icily.

"Well, I suppose we should divide the rugs. You did say you wanted half of them, didn't you?" Colin suggested.

"Half is fair don't you think?"

"Some are big," Colin said, his bright smile following suit and turning a bit cold, "and some are small. As you well know, some are quite valuable and some are rather worthless pretty fakes. Amazing how well they always sell, isn't it? The fake ones, that is."

"Perhaps we should cut them in half," Karen countered, trying her best to get the last word while being careful not to engage Colin any further in a discussion of what was fair or which rugs were valuable.

Arguing with Colin was a losing battle. It was always so easy for him to quote from this source or that in order to bandy his ever-infuriating knowledge about any subject as if it were a club with which to beat her.

"No need to be so full on, as we both know, you've already thought this through," Colin pressed, "and have probably made some tidy little list. I'm surprised the rugs aren't all vacuumed, stacked and labeled: this little pile for Colin and this big one over here for Karen. By the way, who gets the desk?"

"Why don't you take it?" Karen smiled.

"And the chair?"

"Sure, can't have a desk without a chair, can you?"

"So, now we're back to the rugs, aren't we?"

"Yes, the rugs."

"And since you've so generously given me the desk AND the chair, I suppose I should let you have the first go at the rugs. What do you say? You pick one then I pick one, something like that?"

"I thought I'd take all the prayer rugs."

"So," Colin crowed, "I was right. You have thought about it!"

"That will leave you all the bigger rugs including the Luri and the Turkomans. I always thought they were your favorite."

"The often overlooked Turkish prayer rugs. Not so big, because they are made in primitive conditions. Known for their dark brooding blues, reds, browns and blacks, skillfully highlighted with touches of ivory. Beautiful desert gems. I believe you wrote that."

"Correct," Karen said.

She was angry he could so easily find a way to use her own careful work to punish her.

"A fine piece of writing. Clean, clear, and to the point. Very much like you. But there's another line, isn't there? Something about how you and I have been busy these last fifteen years or so gathering together a rather fine collection of Turkish prayer rugs. I believe you also referred to this small collection of rugs, or this collection of small rugs, however it suits you to think about it now, as probably THE foremost collection in the world of such rugs."

"There's hardly what you'd call a 'collection' anymore, since we've had the sale."

"Let me just say the sale was your idea."

"I believe it paid all the outstanding bills with enough left over for each of us to get a start."

"Oh, yes, your 'fresh start.' Another good idea," Colin smirked.

Karen chose to ignore Colin.

"The two largest Turkomans and the dozen or so Luri are easily worth as much as the thirty smaller Turkish rugs I'm taking. Of course, there are three-dozen or so modern rugs, the 'fakes' as you call them. You just said so yourself that they aren't worth much but sell well. You should do quite nicely for yourself with your half of the rugs."

"Oh, so, you've stacked thirty 'often overlooked' prayer rugs in the corner over there and it has already been decided they are yours and you're taking them and I'm supposed to stand here and be gracious?"

"Look, I believe, if you want to be honest about what we are doing here today we need to put it all out on the table. Correct me if I'm wrong. You are the one who is leaving me which makes me, not you, the aggrieved party. Correct?"

"Is that what this is all about?" Colin said, getting up from the edge of the desk and walking across the room to the neat pile of prayer rugs Karen had, in fact, vacuumed and stacked neatly in the corner. "About you being the aggrieved party? And, somehow, this aggrieved state gives you the right to take what you want without asking?"

"Why don't you ask Lisa, or is it Elise? I can never keep their names straight. Which one did you leave me for?"

"So, this is your chance to hurt me, is it?"

Karen closed her eyes for a brief moment in order to not scream. Her lawyer had told her to be careful about how she handled the splitting of the inventory. He had said it would be difficult. He had suggested it should be worked out on paper, them going through everything together step-by-step in his office under his watchful eye rather than her and Colin sorting through the rugs alone in the store. A collection of antique rugs such as theirs would be a nightmare to split given the rather subjective relative value of the various rugs.

The easiest, of course, would be to take their listed price as their real value and to split them on that basis. It was important, he cautioned her, to keep a level head and be civil if she wanted to get what she deserved. The end of a marriage is one thing, the lawyer had said, with a flick of his wrist as if he were batting away a fly, but the end of a business partnership, now that was blood sport.

Colin refused a proposed meeting to sort through the inventory in her lawyer's office. He didn't have a lawyer. He said he didn't need one and suggested they didn't need hers either to tell them who got which rug. Karen threw a fit when Colin refused, but was secretly glad. She didn't feel like making a civil thing of sorting the rugs. First, she wasn't interested in having half of everything. She wanted only the Turkish prayer rugs. They were the rugs she liked the most and the ones she felt, for whatever reason, were hers. Secondly, she wanted a showdown, a last shouting match of wills to help her make a clean, clear break with Colin so she could go on with her life.

"I believe I'm entitled to the prayer rugs. I was the one who first discovered them and thought we should buy them. No one else was paying much attention to Turkoman prayer rugs before I started collecting them. Everyone else thought the colors were too dark, the ivory touches too garish. I believe you said you didn't like the flowers in them. Thought they wouldn't sell. If I remember correctly, you said they looked like something only an old lady would want for her bedroom."

"People change."

"They do indeed," Karen said, gloating a bit as though she had for once caught him.

"You changed."

"I changed?" Karen shrieked. "I changed?"

"You grew cold."

"Cold? How else could I have survived your little trysts?"

"A touch of forgiveness here or there wouldn't have hurt."

"Forgiveness?"

The thought stunned Karen. She had never even considered forgiveness. Anger, maybe even revenge, but not forgiveness.

"I would have come back. I always came back," Colin offered sheepishly.

"Why? So you could stay around a little longer until you found someone prettier, someone you liked better. Notice, I didn't say loved. I don't believe you know about love."

"Bloody hell."

"Yes," Karen agreed, "bloody hell. That just about covers it for me."

"Well, well, look here," Colin said, jumping off the edge of the desk, his voice bitter with the feigned sound of shock and surprise, "what do you think I found in this tidy little pile of prayer rugs? Could it be an old tattered Turkoman? Could it be the first rug, the start of it all?"

"That's mine."

"Oh ho, says who?"

"I saw it first."

"True. First I saw you and then I saw the rug. Dare I say I saw you and fell in love with you before I happened to notice the rug you were holding? Maybe I fell in love with the rug and felt the only way to get the one was to have the other. Ah, but does any of that really matter? I believe you gave me the rug as a wedding gift, or am I wrong about that too?"

What Karen wanted most right now was the courage to walk across the room and strangle Colin.

"I saw the rug the day before I ever met you."

"But you didn't buy it then, did you, love? You waited. And there were times in our marriage when you said you waited for me. The rug was our little knot of destiny. Isn't that what you used to say?"

The knot of destiny. The Buddhist symbol of good fortune. Karen hated the easy way Colin could always tie things up so tidily. She had grown to despise the name they had chosen for their business, The Knot of Destiny, as if their life together was intertwined in fate. She thought it childish how, whenever Colin signed his name, he let the tail of his neatly cribbed writing flow out into a perfect endless knot.

She had seen the rug the day before she met Colin. She found it in a secondhand shop in the Village. She was a graduate student at CUNY in philosophy and was growing tired of academia. Overall, it was a low time in her life. To top it off, she had just had some stunning argument with her mother over what she was going to do with a degree in philosophy to keep her warm at night. She was feeling sorry for herself, so she went to the Village to get away from her apartment and her life.

She found the lovely Turkoman thrown across an old suitcase in a secondhand store. It was slightly longer than it was wide. The fringe and flat woven skirt were nearly worn down to the edge of the actual rug. There was also a small hole in one corner where it had been repaired: as if someone had either snagged it on a chair leg or caught it on a nail on the floor and sewed it up with a needle and thread. It was dirty and it wasn't the most colorful rug she'd ever seen, but the workmanship seemed rather fine and delicate. There was a small mihrab temple figure centered at one end in a field of burgundy with a pattern on either side where one could place their hands in prayer. It was, Karen was pretty certain at the time, a rather fine example of an old tribal prayer rug. The shop owner had wanted thirty dollars for it. She said she had to think about it. When she came back the next day to buy it, Colin walked through the door just as she picked it up.

"I paid for it," Karen stood firm.

"Yes, I believe that you did. Thirty dollars. So foolish of you. I told you I could have bargained it down to twenty maybe less and we could have used the other ten or so to have a drink together. But you didn't go for it. You paid the thirty dollars and I paid for the drinks. I believe you gave me the rug when we got married. Rather romantic, wasn't it?"

It was romantic. She bought the rug. They had drinks followed by dinner. Before long, the little rug was on the floor at the foot of her bed and Colin was in the bed sleeping with her every night, entertaining her with stories of the bush country of Australia and his adventures traveling the world looking for love. She was hopelessly charmed when he told her that discovering her in the store holding the rug was 'finding his luck.'

Swept away in the softness of his accent, it was easy for Karen to believe there was no reason for her to finish her degree. Graduate school seemed foolish compared with the real world Colin was ready to offer her. When spring semester finished, they decided to follow the luck they'd found together in the little rug and start a business. He sold his watch and his bicycle, she sold her furniture and her books, and they left New York to go trekking across Iraq and Iran buying rugs.

It was the first of many trips together to the Middle East in search of rugs in the bazaars. Colin would bargain with the rug sellers while Karen stood in the shadows and watched the beautiful women who wove the rugs make their way through the stalls carrying their wares. She loved how the gold coins they sewed into their skirts and wore in their dark hair jingled when they walked. They were very different ladies from the black veiled women she saw in the bigger cities making their shy silent ways through the streets. The weavers felt bold and primitive and strong. Sometimes Karen dreamed of them dancing around their campfires singing stories they would later weave into their rugs.

She had wanted to talk to the women, but Colin had warned she should not.

"What would you talk about?" he'd tease her. "The weather?"

"No," she had once said, standing up to him. She said she wanted to talk to them about their lives and the rugs they wove. She wanted to hear their stories so she could understand the tight pulled knots of their beautiful rugs with their dancing colors.

Colin had laughed at her. "They weave the rugs," he had told her, putting his arm around her shoulders as though he were trying to move her away from an oncoming bus, "and we weave the stories that sell them. They have their work. We have ours."

Karen argued with him that the patterns in the rugs were not just patterns but stories, the women's stories. Colin pulled her closer to him, his hand tight against her arm. "Of course," he soothed, "of course, the patterns in the rugs do mean something. You can even believe they're magic if you want to. Magic rugs always sell well."

She had wanted to pull away from his grasp and go running after the women. Perhaps, she thought, they'd teach her how to weave, and she would join them. But she didn't run, she stayed and eventually regretted she'd ever married Colin.

That little seed of regret grew into a loud angry tape that played in her head whenever he corrected something she said or laughed at her or stepped in front of her when a customer came into the shop to look at her beautiful prayer rugs.

"The Knot of Destiny," Colin said, pulling the small prayer

rug from Karen's stack.

"A ridiculous name."

"And what will you call your business, your new life?"

"I'm not sure."

"I doubt that, love."

"The Perfect Rug," Karen almost spit out the words she was so angry he could so easily make her tell.

Colin laughed.

"The Perfect Rug. Our little game. Who started it? Was it you? I believe it was. How we'd lay out all the rugs we'd bought each day in the hotel room and drink cheap wine and eat dates and figs and hard cheese and you'd make up these silly stories about how this woman must have been happy, see how beautiful her stitches are, how rich the garden she's woven."

"They weren't silly."

"Of course they were. That and the ridiculous notion you had that someday you'd find the perfect rug. Are the prayer rugs perfect? Is that why you want them?"

"No."

"And I'm not perfect either, am I? But you thought I was or perhaps I should be and that is why you can't forgive me because somehow you have a stranglehold on perfection."

Karen felt stung by his words. Stung in a way she didn't think he could ever sting her again. God, he was beautiful, she thought. Beautiful and brash and so full of himself she was sometimes dazzled by him, and other times she wanted to slap him. She did slap him once, the first time she caught him sleeping with another woman. She slapped him hard across the face and grabbed her purse and coat and started to run for the door, but he grabbed her. He grabbed her tight and he pulled her close, so close she could feel his breath on her face when he spoke.

"Where would you be now, without me?" he had hissed. "With your books in your make-believe life of right and wrong? I showed you the world. I gave you a life. You'll never leave me."

She didn't leave him then because she had nowhere to go. But, all of that was a long time gone: like the women in their bright-colored skirts and their jingling gold coins. The caravans were long gone, as well as the slow-moving camels laden down with rugs, the bright crackling campfires, the wild dancing and storytelling.

Karen quit going on the buying trips once she knew for sure Colin was cheating on her. She quit going when the caravans disappeared and the rugs began to be woven in the city courtyards and the crowded factories where children tied the knots and the women dragged them home after their long day of work. There was nothing beautiful about the work they did. At the end of the day, the children and the mothers fell asleep in their cold beds without a fire to dance around or stories to tell or songs to sing.

The rugs they made were no longer magic. Karen knew this to be true. But she never quit believing that the women who once strutted boldly through the bazaars, their bright skirts swishing and their gold coins flashing, were not the kind of women who would sit day after day weaving someone else's stories into their rugs.

"No one is perfect," Karen said looking at Colin's sad lined face, "I want the prayer rugs because I can pick them up by myself without any help from you and I can put them in the back of my car and drive away. I want them because I think they're beautiful. I want them because they're soft when I touch them and when I press my face against them they still smell of smoke and camels and desert winds and the earthy sweat and spice of the bazaar. That's all, Colin, really, that's all."

"We were good partners, weren't we?" he whispered surprised by how beautiful she was and how much he liked to look at her face.

"Wonderful partners," Karen said, and she meant it.

"You should have this rug," he said, holding out the small

tattered Turkoman she'd found in the Village fifteen long years ago when he first saw her. "But it will cost you."

"How much?" she asked, relieved to be free at last of her anger and her resentment.

"A story. One last story, please," Colin teased.

"So nice to hear you say please."

"I regret I didn't say it more often. I regret..."

"Shhh," Karen silenced him, her fingertip touching her lips. "Let me see this rug you're talking about."

Colin held out the Turkoman to her as if he was showing it to her for the first time. As he gave it to her he let his hand brush against hers.

Karen studied the rug. She held it out in front of her before she spread it on the floor. She smoothed it flat with her hands.

"I see a mihrab here, a place of prayer. The weaver is a new bride. This is part of her bride price and her mother has told her to make a prayer rug. The girl is not afraid. She loves the man who wants to marry her. Her prayers have been answered. She does not need to weave a prayer rug. But she does what she is told. See how clever she is, she has woven a mihrab in the midst of a garden. The flowers are like the ones she's seen in the bazaar in the other rugs of the other young women who come to sell their woven stories. But these flowers are different. They are not tight and angular like the flowers in the rugs her mother and sisters weave. They cannot be mistaken for anything but flowers. They are flowers bursting with color and the perfume of promise. She has woven a sun-soaked garden in full bloom. She is dreaming about the children she will carry. See the jagged peaks she has woven like a fence around her flowers? They are the mountains she and her husband will climb. The mountains are steep and there are many of them but they are beautiful. See how tight and sure her stitches are here? She surrounds herself with mountains because she feels strong. She will not be disappointed if the children do not come. She will not lose faith if the winter is cold."

Karen paused for a moment before going on.

"See the hatchlu cross she has woven in the enter of her rug? The cross is the trouble she will have in her life. The rug will help her carry her troubles."

"Yes," Colin said, stepping close to the rug, wanting ever so much to lean down and bury his face in the mushroom smell of Karen's dark brown hair.

"She knows you cannot have dreams without troubles. Good comes with bad."

"Is it really a prayer rug?"

"Yes," Karen said, letting her hands play across the close-cropped pile of the silky carpet, "and no. Everything we weave in our lives is held together with prayer. Just because a rug has a mihrab, however, does not necessarily mean it is a prayer rug. It may be just a rug. This one could have been used as a tent flap, to keep out the cold of the evening. It is nearly square now because the fringe is gone, but it was once a bigger rectangle. It could have been a tablecloth or even a saddle blanket. But, it is still a prayer rug because the weaver has woven her dreams into it. Her dreams are like prayers. Her prayers of hope and need, prayers of thanks, prayers of confession, and prayers..."

"Of forgiveness?" Colin asked.

"Prayers of forgiveness," Karen said, brushing her hands against the rug one last time as though she could wipe the slate clean for a new story to be woven.

"It was a good story," Colin said quietly, kneeling to roll the small rug and place it on the pile with the others. "The rug is yours. You saw it first and now you've paid for it a second time."

"Could you help me?" Karen asked, pointing to the rugs.

"Surely," Colin said, grabbing an armful of rugs from the top of her stack to take out to her car.

"We were good partners," Karen hesitated, holding the door, "weren't we?"

"We could still be," Colin said. "Business partners, that is."

"Not enough for me."

"No worries," Colin said as he put the rugs into the trunk of her car. He flashed her that easy smile of his and turned to go back into the store to get the rest of them.

"No worries," Karen echoed, realizing the worries had always been hers to carry, not his.

"Here's the lot," Colin said, turning from the trunk of her car to face her, rubbing his hands down the front of his jeans as though he was fifteen again and didn't know what to do with them. "Would you like a few of the others?"

"This is plenty," Karen said, extending her hand. "Thanks for everything."

"I really believed it was meant to be," Colin said taking her hand.

"It was," Karen said, pulling him close to her so she could kiss him one last time on the cheek before she left.

"I'm sure it was."

CHAPTER 10

2002
THE OLDER SISTER

The sidewalk was jammed with people waiting to get in. The front door was open and there were two tables on either side of the door. The people seated at the tables were taking names, credit information, and issuing numbers. There were people with clipboards wearing official-looking dark green shirts milling around both inside and out and people posted at both the front and side doors.

"You must have a number to enter," the tallest and most important-looking of them all called out over the crowd. "You cannot bid without a number."

Susan had no intention of bidding. Her heart skipped a short beat when she got up to the man at the desk.

"Name," he asked, "and credit card."

"For?"

"In case you bid on something but don't show up to get it. Also, if your check bounces, we charge you for it."

"What if I don't intend to bid?"

"Then why did you come?"

"Here," she said, snapping her credit card down onto the table for him to copy her name and number.

"Ever been to a Federal bankruptcy auction?" he asked, sliding her credit card back to her along with a number printed on a card.

"No."

"You should be careful with this number. It could get you into trouble."

Susan slipped her credit card back into her wallet and took the number 231 and walked quickly past the man checking bidders at the doorway.

Once she was in the room, she slipped the number into her purse. She didn't care much for trouble. Not today. Not ever.

She wasn't at all like her brother.

"How could you do this?" she had screamed at Alan when he told her.

"I didn't DO it, it happened."

"Happened?"

"You know I have a hard time paying attention to details."

"Bills aren't details. Taxes aren't details. Money, Alan, is not a detail."

"Enough," he said pushing up his glasses and resetting a smile on his face. "Do you want to know about the rug or not?"

"I can't do this."

"It will be good for you. Give you something to talk about with your friends. You do have friends, don't you?"

"Yes, and I have fun too," she said, closing the wound Alan was always digging at, that she didn't have any fun in her life, any friends, only work, "and money in the bank."

"Touché, my little sister, touché. Now, the rug."

It was, Alan explained, his hands drawing a tight precise picture of it in the air as he spoke, the only real thing in his store. The rest was junk: copies that looked good and sold well to people who didn't know any better.

"I want you to have it, but I can't give it to you because, you see, they made me leave and lock everything up. On my way out, I took the tag off the rug and threw it on the floor in the back room. The feds and all their happy worker bees have been very busy these last couple of weeks numbering things and moving them around, all the time stepping on the rug with their dirty little shoes."

"Great."

"No, this is good. The dealers will come. Some serious. Others looking for a killing. They'll be moving fast, picking up whatever they can at a bargain. They know most of it is worthless but they also know what sells. Some rich biddies will come too, thinking they're smart to get in on the ground floor before they have to pay big bucks for it from their decorators. Everyone will know everyone else. It will be like a party without cocktails. Most dealers won't bid much against other dealers, unless they've got a client looking for something particular. They will, however, bid against the old ladies and the old ladies will keep bidding if they think whatever it is they want will match their sofa. And frankly, since none of this is going into my pocket I could care less if they gave the stuff away.

"In any case, it will be great fun and I'll be missing it. With luck no one will notice the rug. It long ago lost its skirt and fringe and is not in great shape so the snobs in the crowd will pass on it. The auctioneers will barely mention it, just hold it up and hope it goes fast because they've got lots more to sell. I figure they'll do the back room last. There are a few other good pieces there, a seventeenth-century temple scroll, and a pretty hand-carved wooden screen from Thailand, all much too showy and hard to hide or I'd say go after those too. Oh well.

"The auctioneers will make the big dealers wait for the good pieces. They want to hold the dealers in the house as long as they can. They need them there to drive the prices up a little when the blue hairs start bidding for the chandeliers."

"I don't have money to throw away."

"Throw away! Pa-lease. This isn't throwing away, Susan. This is investing."

"How much?"

"It's a Turkoman Prayer Rug, early 1900s, authentic, pretty worn around the edges. Beautiful reds, blacks and rich tans. Fine, fine weave, the front like rough old velvet, the back like a church vestment needlepoint. The designs are small and delicate. It's very subtle."

"How much?"

"Depends on how you handle it."

The front of the store was packed with people. There was no air conditioning, just a fan perched on top of a wooden ladder blowing at high speed. The shop was a mess. Everything had been pulled off of the shelves and numbered then piled onto various tabletops, chair seats, shelves and the floor. The place felt dirty. Susan was secretly glad Alan wasn't there. He would have hated it.

"We'll start downstairs," the man in charge shouted over the pulsing whir of the electric fan, "then work our way up."

Susan didn't follow the others when the auctioneer led the crowd down the stairs. Instead, she walked to the back of the shop to look for the rug. Sure enough, just like Alan had said, it was there, lying on the floor, dusty with footprints. It didn't have a tag.

"Looking for some excitement?" the man behind her asked, his mouth brushing slowly against her ear when he spoke to her.

"Michael," Susan gasped, catching his hand as it slipped around her waist. Michael was Alan's "other." Other or not, Susan had told him on more than one occasion that he was too beautiful to be gay and to please remember her if he ever changed his mind.

"I see Alan sent you," he said, twirling an invisible mustache.

"And you?"

"Of course."

"For?"

"The temple scroll. Don't look," he warned, "they're watching. And you?"

Susan nodded her head toward the small rug on the floor. Michael shifted his weight, took two steps forward, flipped the edge of the rug over with the toe of his shoe, flipped it back again and turned to face her.

"What do you think?" she asked.

"Turkoman. Old, authentic. A little worn, but better for the wear. Beautiful colors, rich-looking. It'll draw some bidders. So will the scroll. Let's hope this takes a little time and they never turn on the air conditioning. A little heat and boredom might drive some of these sharks away from our treasures."

The bidding was fast. There was no minimum sale price. The lowest bid accepted was five dollars but the auctioneer indicated he liked the sound of twenty or even twenty-five better. Whenever anyone raised their number or nodded their head to indicate a higher bid, one of the men with a clipboard called out a sharp, "hup, hup," as though he was driving dogs through the snow.

"Makes the corporate lawyer in you nervous, doesn't it?" Michael whispered, squeezing her waist playfully. "Better keep that number down."

"Municipal bond lawyer, not corporate lawyer."

"Don't talk so sexy if you don't mean it."

"I couldn't help him, Michael."

"He didn't ask for help."

"This feels so dirty."

"He's over it. Moving on. Sent us to get the good stuff. He's that kind of guy."

"Jesus, what a lot of junk."

"You mean to tell me you intend to pass up that clean flawless washable synthetic oriental copy over there for this raggedy moth-eaten scrap of wool rug that isn't even big enough to put under a decent-sized coffee table?"

"I didn't say I was buying it."

"You're here aren't you?"

"For the experience."

"You don't get out much, do you?"

"Don't believe everything Alan says about me."

"Only the part about you being a hard-working upstanding lawyer out to save humanity by building better hospitals, schools and roads."

"Well at least I'm not some old sleazebag ambulance-chaser."

"Give it time."

"Nice."

"We should have been lovers."

"Your call, not mine."

"Ooohhh, the way you talk. How could Alan say you were so, so—"

"So, what?"

"Tight-assed."

"Oh, that's real nice," she said, her eyes flashing.

"Careful. Don't get your number up."

"I can't believe I'm here."

"It's legal. If that's what you're worried about."

"I should probably be worried about Alan."

"He'll bounce."

"Yep," Susan said, letting the heavy taste of the last consonant explode on her lips. She stared at the rug.

The colors were dark, the patterns small and finely worked. It wasn't flashy at all except for the "if you have to ask you're not cultured enough to own it" edge it had to it. It was just the sort of rug one of the firm's senior partners would nail to their wall like a trophy. It was classy, but it wasn't her. Her office was black and white, sleek and polished. She had two framed prints from the Santa Fe Opera. The place had the look she wanted: all business, nothing showy, very straight arrow clean and tidy.

She was just about to tell Michael to get the rug for himself when a woman in a tight faux-leopard miniskirt worked her way across the room and draped herself in one smooth liquid motion around Michael's neck. Susan couldn't help herself. She took a quick hard look at the woman's face to see if there was a hint of a five o'clock shadow, and at her neck to check for an Adam's apple.

Hanging out with Alan and Michael had taught her that only

drag queens look good in leopard. This, however, Susan was pretty sure after close examination, was just a woman dressed up like a drag queen. The skirt made her look cheap.

"Love your new bauble," Michael said, pointing to the four-inch-long diamond-eyed jade jaguar dangling by its tail from the heavy pounded gold chain resting around her neck.

"Don't you just love older men," she said giving the jaguar and her breasts a little shake.

"Linda," Michael said, stepping back so she could take a minute to untangle herself from him, "I'd like you to meet Susan, Alan's older sister."

"I can't tell you," Linda said, extending her hand, "how upset I was to hear Alan was having trouble."

"So upset," Michael added, "that you brought the van?"

"My son Edwin has opened a shop."

"Linda's a decorator," Michael offered. "She and Alan go way back."

"Way back," Linda chimed in. "He has such a good eye. Impeccable taste. All my clients loved him. He called me last week. Told me not to miss the sale."

"And what else did he tell you not to miss?" Michael teased.

"That little hand-carved screen for one thing. Alan said it reminded him of me. There are, of course, some other things I thought I'd buy: some mirrors and small end tables for Edwin's shop, and perhaps a few gaudy knick-knacks for my clients. But I do like the looks of that screen. How's the bidding?"

"Low," Susan piped in.

"The economy is just dreadful," she said with a little the click of her false fingernails, "no one's got any money right now."

"Except for that sweet old daddy of yours," Michael said, nodding to the jaguar.

"He's a smart boy," Linda said with a wink. "He always has money to spend on me."

The auctioneer and the bidders came up from the basement

and moved to the front of the large showroom where the auction would take place.

"Before we start with the chandeliers," the auctioneer called out jovially to the crowd behind him, "we're going to sell off the contents of the office. Do I hear five dollars for a desk? Ten? Fifteen?"

The desk went for ten dollars, the chair five, and the whole cabinet full of office supplies for fifteen. Susan wondered if before he left Alan had rid the files of any evidence of other sins of omission. Or, if he dabbled in a little petty theft by sticking a box of paper clips or a fist full of ballpoint pens in his pocket when they made him leave and lock up.

The three of them stood together silently listening to the auctioneer move from the stuff in the office to the window treatments, and finally to the Waterford-crystal chandelier hanging in the middle of the showroom.

"Well, well," Linda said, her gaze catching the edge of Susan's rug, "as I live and breathe. Alan left us a treasure."

"It's been repaired," Michael offered.

"All the better. Gives it that authentic look. Ought to bring more. Edwin could sell the living be-Jesus out of that thing."

"He's got better than this."

"Better, but his customers are a lot like me: they like the real thing and they like it old," she said, flashing her diamond ring.

"Go buy some gaudy mirrors for Edwin's rich customers," Michael said, giving Linda a playful push, "you don't need that rug. Besides, Susan wants it."

"Did Alan send you?" Linda asked.

"No," Susan lied, "I'm a collector."

"You look like a lawyer to me," Linda said, eyeing her coolly.

"No law against collecting, is there?"

"Of course not," Linda smiled.

She gave Michael a quick peck on the cheek.

"If you all will excuse me, it's time for me to go to work."

"You could have told a better lie," Michael suggested as Linda walked away.

"I could have told her about the temple scroll," Susan said, deciding to abandon Michael for the moment and wander off.

While she listened to the auctioneer casting his singsong spell on the crowd, Susan stood in the doorway and watched the rug. Michael was working the crowd while staying a careful distance from the temple scroll, always moving in such a way so that everyone he spoke to would be forced to have their back to it.

While she listened to the bidding and half-watched Michael's little dance, her eyes wandered around the tight clean pattern of the border on the rug. It had a Greek-key look to it, and on either side of this pattern were wide bands of woven Vs, like the quilt pattern her grandmother used to make she called Flying Geese. The wide-angled black and red Vs repeated themselves down either side of the rug like wings in flight. Susan wanted to touch the rug, to feel its smooth worn fibers.

If she bought it, she thought to herself, she wouldn't put it in her office. She'd keep it at home.

"You want it don't you?" Michael said, sneaking up on her again.

"What?" Susan said, startled.

"You'd think your eyes would find the patterns busy, bothersome, but they're not. They're restful, almost prayerful, like an invitation to sit down and meditate. That's why people love them."

"I don't think I care for the color," Susan said idly.

"Really?" he said as he moved away to talk to someone else, in order to divert their attention from the scroll he wanted.

Susan watched Linda work her way around the room hugging this person and chatting up that person while she deftly used the numbered card in her hand to place her bids.

"Tell me about the rug," Linda commanded as she moved into the doorway where Susan was standing.

"It's an old rug," Susan replied curtly.

"Pretty is as pretty does," Linda said, using her left hand to straighten the clasp on her necklace, hovering over the jaguar just long enough for Susan to get a good look at the clump of diamonds on her ring finger. "My old man's a lawyer. Big time. Big enough to not care what people think and old enough to know people are just people and nice is an easy thing to be. I say the rug is Turkoman. Old, maybe even early 1900s. Not too many rugs its age still around. It's of a common enough design, but probably the best of its time. Beautiful workmanship and except for the tiny touch of orangish red, the rest are natural dyes. It's worn a little in such a way that indicates it may well have been used as a prayer rug. Praying five times a day can wear anyone out. Looks like it's been repaired once or twice, but nicely repaired, museum-quality repaired. That tells me two things. It's good enough to be taken good care of and rich people once owned it. Rich people don't get rich by making stupid mistakes."

"I didn't mean to be rude."

"Alan made mistakes mostly because he never has cared much about getting rich."

"You're right about that," Susan laughed.

"So, tell me about the rug."

"I like the columns of triangles. They remind me of flying geese."

"Like the quilt pattern," Linda said, letting her eyes wander over the carpet. "Prayer rugs can hypnotize you. They're fascinating. I've got two or three just like this one, not as old or as fine, of course. Keep them scattered around my house. Eye candy, my husband calls them, and he's right. If there ever was a magic carpet you know it would look just like this."

"Alan sent me. Told me he wanted me to have the rug."

"Alan must like you."

"He's my brother."

"Listen, my brother's okay, but I'd never cut him in on

something like this. This rug can take you places. You can feel it."

"Hmm," Susan said, nervously playing with the bidding card in her hand.

"What's your number?"

"My number?"

"On your card. I always look for something with a little game in it. Like 111 because the numbers add up to three and there are three numbers in 111. Things like that make me feel lucky."

"231," Susan said, holding up her card.

"Good enough," Linda said, "two plus one equals three, there are three numbers. Two, three, one is like one, two, three with one of the numbers jumping ahead. That's good enough. Gonna bid?"

"What would I do with it?"

"Well," Linda laughed, "looking at you with your wallpaper suit it's a safe bet that you'd never hang it in your office. Maybe you'd hide it in your bedroom or throw it under a coffee table hoping no one would notice it. Who knows, maybe you'd do something wild like pray on it."

"What would I pray for?" Susan said with a nervous laugh.

"I don't know, honey," Linda said, flashing a smile along with her diamond ring, "maybe you'd pray for a sweet old daddy like mine. That's your business. Mine is to find out if you want that rug because if you don't, I do. I've got prayers a mile long I want answered."

Susan rested her eyes again on the rug. The rich dark red of the weave was warm and inviting. She let her eyes ride along the neat marching rows of patterns, falling into their hypnotic twists and turns. It was, like Linda had said, eye candy. But it was more than that, and for a moment Susan felt the oddest flicker of a notion the rug had been places and just might be magic.

"What's it worth?" she asked.

"Hmmm," Linda said straightening the jaguar on its chain, the fingernails on her left hand clicking against its hard polished surface, "worth about a couple hundred bucks to me. No matter what I paid for it, I'd get a couple hundred more from someone else. Then again, could be worth more, a whole lot more, depending on why you want it or where you think it might take you."

"Like that diamond ring?" Susan said, nodding to the rock on Linda's hand.

"More or less," she answered, throwing back her head and shaking out an easy rolling laugh. "You've got yourself a lucky number there, 231."

Susan lifted the number and took a long hard look at it.

"You gonna bid?"

"Maybe."

"Here's what I'm thinking," Linda said, twisting the ring so the largest diamond sat square on her finger. "I'm thinking we'd be fools to bet against you."

"Yep," Susan said. And she knew, in that moment, the rug was hers.

Roundfire Books put simply, publish great stories. Whether it's literary or popular, a gentle tale or a pulsating thriller, the connecting theme in all Roundfire fiction titles is that once you pick them up you won't want to put them down.